A Kind of Tragic Wedding

Gem Burman

Copyright © 2021 Gem Burman

All rights reserved

The characters and events portrayed in this book are fictitious. Any similarity to real persons, living or dead, is coincidental and not intended by the author.

No part of this book may be reproduced, or stored in a retrieval system, or transmitted in any form or by any means, electronic, mechanical, photocopying, recording, or otherwise, without express written permission of the publisher.

For Mike and Nanna, soulmates reunited.

Contents

Title Page
Copyright
Dedication
Prologue
Chapter 1:	1
Chapter 2:	22
Chapter 3:	43
Chapter 4:	65
Chapter 5:	86
Chapter 6:	104
Chapter 7:	122
Chapter 8:	139
Chapter 9:	164
Chapter 10:	182
Chapter 11:	205
Chapter 12:	222

Chapter 13:	240
Chapter 14:	260
Chapter 15:	285
Chapter 16:	301
About The Author	309
Books In This Series	311

Prologue

Decisions, decisions. We go through life making a lot of them. Some good, some bad. Some of them right, some of them wrong. I've made a lot of bad decisions in my thirty years of life – like the last-minute one to home dye my dress using onion skins the night before my first date with Mr Wonderful, which incidentally led to me almost being blinded in one eye by a toilet air freshener! Then there was that unfortunate egg explosion incident when I'd decided it would be quicker to hard boil eggs in the microwave and learned the hard way.

The thing is, without the ability to see into the future you never can tell in advance if the decision you make will be the right one. Hindsight is all we have and by then it's too bloody late! 'Trust your instincts,' they say. 'Listen to your inner voice,' they say. Well, my inner voice has been responsible for each and every monumental fuck up of my life, of which up to now there have been too many to count. Hmph. And it's not like I can trust my gut either, not when all it's ever told me is to eat more shit!

But now with my wedding to Brian looming on the horizon and the discovery that the love of my life was and still is in love with me for *me* – not just because he's under the illusion of some dodgy love spell – suddenly my entire world has gone batshit, spinning out of control while I stumble about discombobulated, my head telling me one thing and my gut the other.

So now what? Where do I go from here?

Time, as they say, will tell. The trouble is, it's running out.

Chapter 1:

Merry and Shite

The venue stands ready, preened, polished and awash with powder pink. Not a single detail overlooked from the sea of fresh-cut carnations to Mother's fuck-off great hat. Swathes of guests all turned out in their finery are seated, waiting in excited anticipation for the bride's arrival ... *my* arrival.

As the gleaming, ribbon-dressed white Bentley transporting Dad and I draws up outside, my rocketing anxiety hits fever pitch. Dad senses it. He gives me a sympathetic smile and squeezes my hand reassuringly. It doesn't help much.

Taking a deep breath, I exit through the right side of the car, stepping out onto the forecourt of the prestigious country club immersed in a backdrop of hilly woods and surrounded by perfectly manicured lawns that stretch on for miles across the vast estate.

As Brooke totters over and begins gathering up the enormous train of my wedding dress just as we'd rehearsed, it surfaces. As I link Dad's arm and we proceed toward the entrance, it nags away at me. As we stand waiting outside the doors to the grandiose ceremony room, it consumes me. As I begin walking down the white-carpeted aisle in synchrony with the classical music among an air of adoring 'oohs' and 'ahhs', a throng of beaming faces staring at me in adulation, it overcomes me. The music gives way to a highly charged silence and then, as my eyes meet my husband-to-be's, it's crushing me. Killing me. I can't do this!

Desperately overwhelmed and without a word, I turn to run back up the aisle, my anxious gasps carried by the unforgiving echo chamber reverberating across the room as I go. I try to blank out row upon row of open-mouthed faces gawking at me in horror. Then, in what feels like slow motion – as well as the story of my life – I trip over the ball gown skirt of my wedding dress and face-plant onto the aisle carpet with a great thud!

'Doh …. FUCK!'

Whoops, *that* just reverberated about the place too, loud enough for all to hear and be appalled.

I hear a distant male voice I don't recognise.

'But Mrs Bradshaw, I-I always clean them to the best of my ability. I'm really not sure what else I can…'

Followed by a familiar shrill.

'Now, listen to me, Mr Gleam! We have a VIP staying with us – a billionaire businessman from New York. I will *not* have him slumming it in an abode with smeary windows.'

I wake with a jolt, heart pounding beneath the sweaty cocoon of Mother's floral Laura Ashley bedcovers, breathing a sigh of relief upon observing the Brian-shaped mound snoring beside me as I find myself unwittingly privy to Mother's interrogation of the poor prat who cleans her windows.

'Yes, you *did* leave them smeary last time!' she accuses.

'Look, Mrs Bradshaw, nobody else has ever—'

'I couldn't give a jot about anyone else,' she barks. At least she's being honest. 'I have an extremely important social function this evening, so I'm sure you can see the need for windows that shine like new pennies,' she argues loudly out on the driveway, even though it's winter and, therefore, is going to be pitch black when her ghastly guests arrive for her festive soirée tonight.

Ugh, *that* I'd quite forgotten about, what with being otherwise consumed by the dilemma I find myself in. Dan Elliott, only yesterday at the airport, confessing he loves me – the *old* me – just as I'm to marry Brian, who also loves me – the *new* me. Hmm, I know, right! One minute I'm trying to train my subconscious mind into accepting my fate as a doomed spinster, the next it's raining men!

As I lie gazing up at the swirly-patterned ceiling of my parents' spare room, tuning out of Mother's squealy hissy-fit on the driveway, I begin questioning everything. Am I happy with Brian? I mean, truly, madly, deeply? I had always believed that when I married, it would be forever, and forever is a long time – especially when it's spent with the wrong person. Is Brian absolutely, definitely the one? I tell myself he is, but now, in my heart of hearts, I'm not so sure. Particularly as the nasty rasp of his snoring brings me back to reality and I am overcome with this sudden, massive urge to shove him out the bed.

I glance at the bedside clock. 7.28am. There's no such thing as a lie-in at Fairview, the four-bedroomed detached leafy London home of my parents. Not for jet-lagged house guests, not for billionaires, possibly not even for royalty. The Queen would have to bloody well fit in with Mother's wants and desires!

Mother, as an early bird – a far nicer way to allude to her being one of these hyper types with nothing much to do – simply cannot wait to get up at the crack of dawn in readiness to swan about organising, delegating, smothering and stifling all in her company, not letting a little thing like sleep get in the way of her objectives. This makes anyone else residing at Fairview early risers by default, reinforcing that age-old saying of mine and Dad's that 'Nothing's fair at Fairview'.

Brian seems to have joined the ever-growing list of victims of "the Petunia Bradshaw way" as later on in the morning he corners me in the kitchen to enlighten me on her having burst in on him in his underpants during her rush to needlessly re-stock the spare room's en suite with extra towels.

'Could you maybe ask her to knock next time?' he asks. 'I mean, we're soon to be family, but I'm never gonna be comfortable with your mother seeing my Johnson.'

'God, no!' I agree distantly. 'I'll ... have a word with her.'

'You okay?' Brian asks, his face falling a touch. 'You've been pretty quiet since we got here.'

Shit! Must stop being so obvious.

'Er, yeah. Fine!' I lie, faking a smile. 'Just jet-lagged, that's all.'

'Hmmm, you and me both,' he agrees, pulling me toward him for a smooch just as the devil herself strides in, clutching the post.

'Goodness, *more* Christmas cards! Wherever shall we put them all?' Mother sighs dramatically, feigning exhaustion at receiving such validation of her popularity.

Brian and I pull apart from one another as she launches into a loud, high-pitched verbal checklist of everything she must do before tonight's Arseholes Anonymous meeting. We slip out of the kitchen unnoticed, leaving her reeling off umpteen to-do's while finding homes for the Christmas cards she very possibly wrote out and mailed to herself.

Later, at what is shortly before 7pm, comes the first ding-dong alerting to the arrival of arsehole number one. With a deep, pre-emptive sigh, I revert back to my former position – mouth wide open while applying mascara in the bathroom mirror, as we do.

'You nearly done?' Brian asks, popping his head around the door. 'We should head downstairs, get a drink.'

'Drink! Yes, drink!' I exclaim, recalling the magical boost to coping skills alcohol offers in these situations. 'You wouldn't be a love and bring a glass of something upstairs while I finish up here, would you?' I ask, batting my lids.

When Brian still hasn't returned with that drink after twenty minutes, I conclude that Mother, like a Venus flytrap, has him held hostage, parading him about the front room as star of her show. Hmph! Harbouring a guess that the precedent has been set for the evening, I find myself tiptoeing downstairs on a mission to smuggle contraband back up to the spare room.

Having made it to the kitchen unnoticed, a litre bottle of gin mere inches from my grasp, I freeze as a pair stocky legs clad in mustard corduroys appear at my side, followed by the sudden boom of a deep, plummy voice.

'Ah! If it's not the little entrepreneur herself! How are you, old girl? How are you?'

'I'm very well thanks, and you?' I ask, edging backwards into the kitchen countertop as I find myself trapped by Uncle Gerald's bulky mass. Uncle Gerald whom, up until now, I was never quite sure knew if I existed.

'Jolly good, jolly good! How's life going in the Big Apple, then?' he enquires, his piggy little eyes looking me up and down intently under scary, bushy brows.

'Good, thank you,' I reply, my eyes wildly scanning about the place for an emergency exit.

'You're wasting away, girl! You used to be a right well-covered, buxom thing, didn't you?' he remarks, his eyes boring into my figure.

'Yes, well, much healthier now,' I squeak, swiping the bottle of gin from the countertop and doing a sort of cha-cha slide to the left out of target range.

'All the more buffet for me then!' he declares, rubbing his podgy hands together in delight.

Hm, like you bloody need it!

'Must-mingle-bye!' I chirp in one breath, slinking out of the kitchen and quickly journeying up the wooden hill to Merryville as the nasty shrill of Mother's excitable histrionics reverberates through the house.

Swigging neat gin straight from the bottle while craning my neck, from behind the co-ordinating Laura Asley curtains of the bedroom window, to establish whom else from the long list of pompous undesirables has arrived, I decide to FaceTime Brooke.

'Oh, hey!' she squeals, waving frantically at the screen. 'How'd you guys' trip go?'

'Hey!' I greet her, trying to keep my voice down. 'Well, let's just say it didn't go quite as I'd planned.'

She frowns. 'Oh! Why?'

'Well,' I begin. 'Hang on a sec, why's your voice all echoey? What are you doing? You're not on the toilet, are you?' I probe, puzzled.

'Yeah,' she answers, cool as you like.

'Oh, for God's sake! *Please* tell me it's a number one!'

'No, it's a shit,' she replies matter-of-factly.

'Eww, you're something else!' I grimace, taking a long swig of my smuggled booze.

'Ah, get over yourself, it's not like you can smell it all the way over in…' she trails off, spotting my massive bottle of gin. 'Damn girl, things gotta be bad!' she remarks. 'Whassup?!'

'He was at the airport. Dan was at the airport,' I reply, cautiously eyeing the bedroom door.

'No way! Well, did you speak?'

'Heart to heart,' I nod hastily. 'To cut a long story short, I confessed all about the love spell and he made me feel really silly for thinking it had worked, basically debunked everything I'd said about being worried about bad karma, yada, yada. Then—'

'What? What?!'

'He told me he loved me. Said he always did and still does.'

Brooke gasps, her mouth hanging open in shock. 'Shit!'

'Shit indeed,' I agree, biting my lip.

'He's like, the love of your fucking life! So, what are you thinking?' she asks, mid-strain.

I'm thinking about *him* and nothing bloody but!

'I don't know, Brooke. My head's all over the place. I'm even dreaming about him while my fiancé sleeps beside me for Christ's sake!' I whisper.

'Yeah, what about Brian? The wedding? This is bad!' She sighs, vigorously tearing off sheets of toilet paper one-handedly.

'I know, right!'

'What you gonna do?' she asks, reaching her spare arm behind herself to wipe her arse.

'Ugh, Brooke, please make sure you don't film the tissue ...OH, FOR FUCK'S SAKE!' I yell as it comes into view on my screen in all its soiled glory.

'Well? I gotta make sure I wiped right!' she whines in protest.

'Look, just keep it away from the screen, would you?' I plead, feeling suddenly nauseous just as the bedroom door bursts open, only adding to the feeling.

'*There* you are! Everybody's arriving and you're nowhere to be seen. Really, it's the height of rudeness. Come downstairs at once!' Mother orders through clenched teeth, quickly spying the bottle of gin, tutting in disgust, and snatching it from me in contempt before slamming the door behind her.

'I've got to go,' I sigh to Brooke.

'Hang on, what are you going to do about all this?' she asks, still wiping.

'I really don't know,' I reply with a shrug. 'I'm gonna go now before you stand up to flush. I really don't want to see your—'

Oof, good God. Too late!

Mother spies me hesitantly descending the staircase, grabs me by the forearm and marches me through to the sitting room as though I were five.

'Here's our Elizabeth!' she announces with a silly, grandiose grin, prompting all eyes to fall on me. From the gasps of astoundment that follow, you would think they were meeting Elizabeth II.

'Goodness, I would never have recognised her!' comes a plummy voice to my right.

'She looks like one of those Kardashian sisters,' comes another.

Thanks ... I think!

'Hmph! Definitely a gastric band!' comes a loud and indiscreet murmur from behind me.

I turn to observe the culprit; a shrivelled up old bat in a tweed twinset, perched on the sofa clutching a glass of sherry and eyeing me disapprovingly like a great horned owl.

'They do facelifts as well, you know,' I tell her, observing her nasty face fall in horror. 'I could probably get you a discount.' Although, for this one I imagine it's a bit beyond facelifts and more a case of rebuilding from scratch.

'Doh, the Cumberland sausage rolls!' Mother suddenly screeches over the tail end of my comeback, causing several of her guests to jump out of their skins in shock. Leaving them covering their ears, aghast, she hurries off at speed to the kitchen.

I edge my way through the room of tightly packed toffs over toward the drinks cabinet in the dining room where Dad stands on his tod, uncharacteristically necking rum.

'Stressed?' I remark, reaching for the vodka.

'That obvious, is it?' he replies, taking a lengthy gulp and grimacing slightly as it burns the back of his throat. 'You know I hate all this codswallop,' he adds despondently.

'You should put your foot down, Dad,' I mutter discreetly.

It might have made for good advice for anyone else but, as his contesting look confirms, it's advice wasted on the long-suffering husband of Petunia Bradshaw.

'It's a bit beyond that, love,' he says, shaking his head melancholically. 'I mean … just look at her, she's out of bloody control.' He sighs, gesturing over toward the buffet table where Mother is forcibly grabbing grown adults by the shoulders and organising them into an orderly queue like school children, her long skirt swishing about the place and the shrill of her voice drowning out the festive notes of Shaking Stevens playing merrily in the background.

'Take your point,' I snigger, raising my glass toward him in commiseration.

'Cheers.' He half-smiles as we down our drinks in tandem.

Around a couple of hours in, I'm nicely under the effects of the old bottled Russian water. Just as well since I still haven't managed to get within a mere foot of my fiancé whom has, thus far, been unable to escape the throng of upper-class limpets surrounding him in the front room, hanging off his every word. I stand watching from the dining room in disbelief as they kiss his arse, laughing excessively at anything, comical or not, that comes out his mouth. Really? *This* highly disproportionate level of fawning all because he's a wealthy businessman?

'His shit still stinks, you know!' I find myself longing to yell in scorn, before taking myself off to the buffet table in a huff where I practically swallow whole umpteen fondant fancies.

'Ugh, so good,' I murmur, eyes half closed.

Living under Brian's watchful eye has gone some way to keeping my figure, but it's getting harder and harder to keep Fatty McPhat muzzled. 'More! Gimmee more!' she screams from within me, demanding pork pies, Battenburg, cherry bakewells and umpteen mini yule logs. I pile my plate high as Mother slags off Delia Davenport to anyone who'll listen behind me.

Tuning out, I idly scoff a tempura battered prawn dunked liberally into one of Mother's posh party dips.

'Fuck!' I find myself involuntarily bawling seconds later as the taste hits. I waft the air about my face and pant profusely as whatever it is burns the shit out my mouth. 'Jesus Christ! What the fuck is that?!' I roar, my eyes watering as heads turn sharply. 'Bloody hells bells!'

Mother's face is a picture as she swiftly moves to crank up the volume of the sound system as a means of drowning out all the blasphemy, resulting in a sudden, deafening, distorted eruption of Wizzard's "I Wish It Could Be Christmas Every Day" ringing out about the place. The entire room cover their ears, looking on in horror. She begins singing loudly along to the chorus in the manner of a strangled cat while I race into the kitchen to locate H_2O, the fireman's friend, to put out this hellfire in my mouth.

'What are you trying to do to me?!' Mother hisses through clenched teeth, skidding into the kitchen behind me and looking shadily over her shoulder.

I neck some water, which does nothing to neutralise the burn. Slamming my glass down on the countertop, my eyes darting about frantically for a remedy, my gaze falls upon Mother's Christmas trifle proudly showcased in a long-necked fancy glass bowl. Without thinking, I impulsively slap my hand into the whipped cream topping, scoop a great glob of it and proceed to lap it up like an animal.

Mother yells in shock, her face like a baboon's arse and her eyes bulging in horror as she observes the damage to what was to be her *pièce de résistance*. It seems to do the trick in dampening the hellfire but ignites an altogether different fire within Mother.

'Look what you've done!' she fumes, darting about in all directions, not quite knowing which remedial culinary step to take first. 'What on earth are you playing at this evening?!' she barks.

'Me? It was that fucking dip of yours!' I reply loudly, slurring slightly. 'What in the hell did you put in it, Carolina Reapers?!'

'Language!' she groans through clenched teeth, closing her eyes and covering her face with her hands in exasperation before forcibly shoving me out of the kitchen.

And there was me believing this year's festive shitshow was to be so much more bearable with Brian by my side – or not since he *still* hasn't brushed off his gaggle of admirers.

'Ah, fuck the lotta yer!' I mumble, taking myself upstairs where I throw myself onto the bed with a deep sigh.

I turn to see Brian's pyjamas neatly folded on the pillow beside me and am hit by a sudden tidal wave of rage.

'Ooh look at me, aren't I efficient with my stupid … bloody …poxy … pyjamas!' I sneer babyishly, rolling over and punching them repeatedly as they lay all smug upon the pillow. 'Tell you what, how do you like *this* you pompous, brushed-cotton bastards!' I yell, kicking them and the pillow to the floor.

I freeze in contemplation for a few moments. That felt good, but Christ, I'm essentially conversing – and fighting – with a pair of sodding pyjamas! What kind of a nutter am I?

Bored out of my brain, I snatch my phone from the bedside table where it was charging and, in what I conclude to be behaviour justifiable by Brian's neglect of me in favour of the hoity toity brigade, being under the influence of the old Russian bottled water, and being in spoiled brat mode, I download the Facebook app and re-activate my formerly dormant account. I tell myself it is merely to ease my boredom and pass the time, when in fact the sole purpose of this illicit action is to study Dan Elliott's profile in great depth. My heart begins racing as soon as it loads, and soon I sit swooning at his profile picture.

'You beautiful, beautiful man,' I sigh, welling up as I stroke the screen, trance-like. I know it's pointless and I'm only torturing myself, yada, yada, but while I can't be with Mr Wonderful, I can't be without him either.

Moments later, with scant regard for the enormity of what I'm about to do, I find myself digging out my old SIM card from where it dwells within the discreet inner compartment of my Kate Spade shoulder bag. I jam it into my phone – almost snapping it in the process – and, by some form of a miracle, manage to get it to work ... eventually.

Then, as if on autopilot, I scroll through my contacts, hovering my index finger over "Sexy Pants" before hitting call without really knowing why or exactly what I plan to say to him.

Ah, bugger! It's gone straight to voicemail. Probably a blessing. Or not. Er ... Er ... Hmm.

BEEP!

'Er ... I-love-you-and-I-can't-live-without-you!' I blurt out in one breath before hanging up and throwing my phone across the room in shock. It sails at speed through the air and an apocalyptic clonk follows as it smashes into what is one of Mother's prized, posh china vases, taking a massive chunk out the rim.

'Oh fuck!' I gasp, covering my mouth with my hands in horror just as the bedroom door opens and Brian enters.

'Oh, hey! There you are, babe,' he greets me, his gaze immediately taking a sharp left and falling upon his pyjamas lying in a sorry heap upon the floor. 'Holy moly! What happened to my nightwear?' he asks, hurrying toward it in a panic, scooping it up off the floor and carefully folding it before, God forbid, he is forced to enter the land of nod wearing creased pyjamas.

'Must've fallen off the bed,' I tell him shiftily, briefly recalling myself punching the crap out of them earlier. They deserved it, sitting there all smarmy and perfect!

He frowns. 'You okay, honey? You seem a little tense.'

'No, no. I'm fine,' I tell him, holding onto the drawers for support and trying to focus my eyes to appear less pissed than I am.

He stares at me suspiciously for a few moments. 'Oh shoot!' he exclaims. 'Your mom needs you downstairs. Says it's urgent.'

With Mother's definition of "urgent" markedly different to everyone else's, I'm ninety-nine-point-nine percent sure it won't be!

Uncle Gerald's fat, rosy face lights up at the bottom of the staircase as Brian and I descend it.

'Ah! There you are old chap!' he exclaims, puffing on an enormous cigar and grinning with glee as he throws a colossal arm around Brian's shoulder and steers him into the sitting room. 'We were just debating whether the unemployed should be forced into the armed forces or shot dead.'

Just as I'm briefly entertaining the idea of grabbing Dad's golf brolly from the umbrella stand and inserting the end of it into the arse of those mustard cords disappearing around the corner, Mother lunges forward out of nowhere, grabs me by the shoulder and ushers me into the study, slamming the door behind her.

'What's going on?!' I slur.

'Oh, for goodness sake, not you as well!' she says with a sigh, flailing her arms about the place dramatically.

'What?'

'It's your father, he's drunk!'

'Oh no! Quick! Quick! A fully grown adult has decided to let his hair down and enjoy a drink at Christmas!' I mock sarcastically.

'This is *not* the time for lower-class wit', she replies. 'He's out there making a ruddy fool of himself! Staggering about telling people to pull his finger and then ... and then ...'

'Farting?' I laugh.

'Don't use such ghastly vocabulary, dear. I think the proper term is breaking wind. Now, I want you to help me get him upstairs and out of the way of the guests,' she demands through clenched teeth. 'I simply cannot have everyone at the country club getting to know about your father's debauchery.'

'He's a bloody grown man, Mother,' I say in protest, 'you can't just banish him off to bed.'

'I think you'll find I can jolly well do as I please!' she hisses. 'My reputation is at stake! Now come on, he was out in the conservatory last I saw, terrorising the female guests,' she barks, grabbing me and shoving me out of the study.

We step into the conservatory where Dad is busy twirling around a giggly, ageing blonde along to Wham's "Last Christmas".

'Woohoo! Yeah, baby!' he yells, draping her across his arm.

I slowly turn my head to look at Mother beside me, who is visibly wobbling with rage.

'Desmond!' she barks. 'Put her down at once!'

'Oh, come here, yer crabby old cow!' he slurs, grabbing her by the waist and dragging her toward him to dance.

Her head jerks violently, the rest of her seizing up in protest as he throws her around. I put my hand to my mouth and stand laughing my arse off.

Later, with Mother busy hurriedly packing off the last of the toffs into the chilly December night air before they can witness any further carnage, I find myself on all fours in the main bathroom upstairs stuck in that God-awful limbo where you want to be sick but you're not quite ready. Fuck knows where Brian is, probably in bed with Uncle Gerald.

Suddenly, the door crashes open, Dad stumbles in retching loudly and proceeds to throw up in the sink beside me. I can hear Mother's urgent footsteps thundering up the stairs over the din of Dad's groaning.

'Will you stop making those vulgar noises?!' she hisses, bursting in and doing a double take. 'Oh no!' she wails, spotting the vomit plastered all over the sink. 'After all that effort I went to to shine the taps!'

Chapter 2:

Nightmare Before Christmas

'Honey!' comes Brian's voice as he gently shakes me awake. 'Honey, wake up, it's your cell phone.'

I open one eye and peer around the room, slowly coming to.

'Ugh, what?' I yawn, rubbing at my eyes.

'Your cell phone was ringing. It rang off twice now.'

I glance at my phone on the bedside table beside me and freeze in horror as I observe two missed calls from "Sexy Pants" displayed on the screen. Fuck! Oh fuck! I only went and left the old SIM card in it in my drunken state last night!

'Who was it?' Brian asks, springing up out of bed and undertaking his usual morning stretches.

'Er, unknown number. Probably a cold caller,' I tell him, going all stiff. More like a hot caller – a very hot caller indeed.

'Ah,' he mutters. 'And how are we feeling this morning?'

'Headache,' I groan, placing my phone back down on the bedside table.

'Well, it goes with the territory,' he remarks, his tone laced with disapproval. 'If you can't do the time, don't do the crime.'

'Oh, don't. You're beginning to sound just like Mother,' I mumble, in no mood for Brian's sensible life coaching.

I freeze in shock as my phone starts ringing again.

'Wow, somebody really wants you,' Brian remarks.

You don't know the half of it, mate!

I sit staring at him, growing pinker with every second it continues to ring.

He frowns. 'You not gonna get that?'

I move to answer it, observing "Sexy Pants" as the caller. As a knee-jerk reaction, I deliberately knock over the glass of water that was resting on the bedside table.

'Oh, shit!' I exclaim in feigned shock as my phone essentially drowns in the spillage.

Brian grimaces. 'Now, that's exactly why I never keep water at the bedside.'

I make a non-committal noise in reply, caring

far less about the phone and feeling more relieved at having escaped what was a spectacularly close call.

'I'm gonna go shower,' Brian announces, pecking me on the lips before venturing off into the en suite bathroom, leaving me counting my lucky stars.

*****

Later at the breakfast table I make a very easy guess that Dad is in the doghouse, if Mother's giving him the silent treatment together with her cat's arse pout is anything to go by. I've never known the place so quiet.

'How are you feeling this morning then, Dad?' I ask, trying my very hardest not to laugh as he peers guiltily over the top of his newspaper like a naughty child.

'Not bad, Lilibeth. Not bad,' he replies softly, clearing his throat before immediately re-immersing himself in the news.

Mother narrows her eyes at him as though silently plotting his death.

'It's Christmas Eve!' I exclaim jovially in an attempt to lift the atmosphere.

Nobody answers and the staunch silence – other than for the periodic annoying gulping sound Mother makes when swallowing her tea and the crinkling of Dad's newspaper – continues, suggesting that Dad and I are very much on the naughty list this year.

Brian, however, earns himself another ten thousand brownie points from Mother and the highest possible ranking on the nice list as he later joins us at the table and announces he'd like to treat us all to a festive lunch at an exclusive restaurant in Knightsbridge. All at once, gone are the staunch silence and cat's arse pout and, in their place what resembles a mad-eyed grinning Cheshire Cat on crack!

'Oh, how wonderful!' she roars. 'Knightsbridge on Christmas Eve. And it'll be the one restaurant I can be sure Delia Davenport has never dined in.'

Honestly, if I hear that woman's bloody name once more, I think I'll spontaneously combust!

With Dad and I both strictly on mineral water, the festive lunch proceeds without incident. That is, until we arrive back home and I spot Mr Wonderful's unmistakably unique car – a souped-up bright blue Nissan GTR complete with massive spoiler – parked a little way up the street. Oh, shit! My blood runs cold, and I go all stiff as I picture the Cheshire Cat spotting him and having kittens, particularly if the neighbours, God forbid, should chance upon the sound of that exhaust.

Dad pulls into the driveway and I hang back as

we exit the car, letting the others who are knee-deep in conversation about politics proceed into the house first. I hear the reverberation of Dan's car door closing nearby as I peer cautiously over my shoulder. I glance back toward the front door in panic to see it's now closed. Charming! Does anyone around here know I exist? Other than for Mr Wonderful, of course.

I hurry back down the driveway and venture out onto the street where the conifer trees framing the driveway conceal me beautifully from view of the house.

'What are you doing here?' I hiss in panic as he approaches. 'Mother will go spare!'

'I had to see you,' he tells me sincerely, letting loose that throng of hyperactive butterflies in my stomach which seem to respond only to the command of his voice. 'That voicemail you left...'

Ugh, that!

'I was drunk,' I quickly excuse.

'You sounded pretty sincere to me,' he counters, gazing at me knowingly. 'Look, I feel the same! I can't stop thinking about you, Lizzie.'

'Dan, I'm engaged to be married,' I remind him.

He nods despondently. 'But it's not too late. There's still time to back out,' he says, as though it were the simplest task in the world.

'I can't, Dan. It's gone too far with Brian. I have a business and a whole new life back in the US. Everything's booked. Mother's gone and bought her sodding hat! I ... can't break his heart. I just can't.'

Dan takes hold of both my hands, rubbing my wrists tenderly with his thumbs. 'But you can't live your life for other people, Lizzie', he says, his voice taking on a serious tone. 'It's not a drill. This is it. You get one life. One shot! You have to live for *you*.' He holds my gaze, letting go of my left hand and rummaging in the pocket of his jeans before dropping to one knee on the pavement.

'Marry me, Lizzie,' he says, opening the ring box to reveal an engagement ring of far lesser proportions than Brian's rock already showcased on my wedding ring finger, but one utterly priceless when I think of the all millions of times I've dreamed of nothing else but this moment.

I gasp, clasping my hand to my mouth in shock. 'But ... but ... you said marriage was a hell of a long way off in your life plans, that time in the Cotswolds,' I remind him as he gazes up at me, lighting a fire within my soul with those eyes of his.

'That's what I believed at the time, but, well, you changed my mind,' he tells me, looking down at the ring. He takes it out of its box and holds it out to me. 'It was my nan's,' he reveals. 'My other nan,' he quickly adds, as though seeing the image of Crabby Gran at that shitshow BBQ appearing at the forefront of my mind. 'I've held onto it for years. Always knew I was going to give it to my future wife. I guess I've been waiting for the right person all this time,' he says, beginning to well up slightly.

'Oh, Dan, I...I ...'

'Think about it. Please just think it about it, at least,' he says, just as Dad appears at the end of the driveway behind us, causing us both to jump out of our skins in fright.

Shit!

Dan quickly rises to his feet and discreetly puts the ring box back into his pocket as Dad approaches.

'Oh, er ... hello, Des,' he calls over to him. 'I um —'

'He came to wish me a happy Christmas,' I quickly interject.

Dad smiles and nods, reaching out to shake Dan's hand. He might be a total doormat, pinned helplessly under Mother's domineering thumb, but he's not stupid.

'Merry Christmas, Dan.' Dad smiles at the two of us. 'We'd better be getting back inside, your mother's doing mulled wine and homemade

made mince pies.' He winks, whistling casually as he strolls off back up the driveway.

Dan leans forward and pecks me on the cheek. 'I love you,' he whispers. 'You know where I am.' Squeezing my hand, he adds, 'Merry Christmas.'

I nod, numbly. 'Merry Christmas, Dan,' I reply in a daze, watching as he turns and jogs off up the street toward his car.

Dad stands holding open the front door, a knowing look on his face as I ascend the driveway walking like a newly born foal – a consequence of both the Dan-effect and my still reeling from the illicit second marriage proposal which Dad may or may not have been privy to.

I enter through the door shiftily.

'Ah, *there* you are! What on earth were you doing outside all this time?' Mother shrills, breezing into the hallway like a tornado.

'She dropped an earring out on the drive,' Dad tells her before I can speak. 'I was helping her look for it.'

I shoot him an appreciative look as Mother, presumably having bought it, bursts into an opera-like rendition of "We Wish You a Merry Christmas", slinking off back into the kitchen.

'Where's Brian?' I ask Dad.

Before he can answer, I hear a deep cough coming from the cloakroom toilet beside us. Oh!

I sit staring vacantly into space as the lights twinkle softly on the Christmas tree and the fire sparks and crackles within the hearth. My glass of mulled wine rests untouched upon the table bedside me as the hum of Mother, Dad and Brian's cosy chat ebbs away to somewhere in the distant background.

How did my former boring and mundane life of singledom come to this? Jeez! It's like that saying about spending forever waiting for a bus, then two come along at once. You almost feel guilty as both chug up alongside you – well, at least I do – not quite knowing which to give your custom to. One of them is destined to miss out, but it's hardly a big deal. They'll be on their way again in seconds and it'll be business as usual. If only things were that simple in my case, only we're not talking lumps of metal here, we're talking people – *real* people – with feelings.

My mind races at a zillion miles per hour. How can I possibly marry Dan? How can I not marry Dan? Brian loves me and I love him … and Dan. Doh! What about the wedding plans and all the money we've spent? What about my business in the US?

What about Brooke? I can't hurt Brian! I can't hurt Dan!

And, what is perhaps the most unnerving prospect of all – Mother's reaction if I should opt to ditch my billionaire fiancé for an airport chauffer with 'nothing to offer me' and 'nothing between the ears'.

Suddenly, I've come over incredibly nauseous. I rise shakily from my seat and leave the room, heading out to the garden while Brian enthrals Mother with his fireside tale of once having bumped into Harrison Ford on the way out of some New York hotel.

The cold December air bites as I trundle down to the garden shed for some deep contemplation. Minutes later, with my having contemplated little more than how many spiders I might be keeping company with, Dad pops his head around the shed door.

'Are you alright, love?' he asks with a frown.

'I'm fine, thanks,' I lie, the universal go-to answer regardless of whether you're at rock bottom or on top of the world. 'How did you guess I'd be here?' I ask, glumly.

'Well, it's the first place I come to when I want to hide from your mother ... which is often,' he chuckles, pulling up an upturned bucket and plonking himself down beside me.

After a brief silence, he sighs.

'I know how you feel about him,' I says.

I slowly turn to look at him in surprise.

'Dan,' Dad adds, raising his brows.

'Ugh, it's all such a mess,' I groan, burying my head in my hands.

'I know,' he soothes.

'Then … You know about … you know that he …'

'Yes, love. I sort of put two and two together when I saw him knelt in front of you on the pavement outside. There's not much else it could have been … unless you were knighting him!' He laughs. 'Besides, I knew it was on the cards, anyway.'

'You *what?*'

'Him proposing to you,' Dad says, clearing his throat as though there's more to come. 'That time he came here asking after you, while you were in America …'

'Yes, yes,' I say, nodding enthusiastically.

'Ah, poor chap was desperate to track you down.' He sighs thoughtfully, pulling a clump of soggy leaves from the sole of his shoe. 'He asked my permission to propose,' he adds, dropping the bombshell.

'He d-d-did?' I stutter in shock.

Dad gives a solemn nod, confirmation that Dan had wanted to marry me long before Brian did.

Ah, shit! If I hadn't raced off to America, I would be married to Mr Wonderful this second. I would be Mrs Elliott, for real! How annoyingly butterfly effect!

'So, what did you say?' I probe further.

'I told him that unless he was planning to marry me, he didn't need my permission. My little girl will marry who she wants to marry.' Dad smiles, his words in stark contrast to Mother's position on the matter.

Frustrated, I ask, 'Why on earth didn't you tell me sooner? It would've all been so much simpler back then, before Brian.'

'Well, you were adamant that you needed a new start, love. I didn't want to complicate things for you. Besides, I rarely get the chance to speak to you without your mother hovering over my shoulder and I thought it best she didn't know.'

He thought right! From my wealth of experience, the less Mother knows about my personal life, the bloody better.

'Oh, Dad, what am I gonna do?' I sigh, fiddling anxiously with my enormous engagement ring.

'You do what *you* want to do, love,' he tells me sincerely. 'Don't be worrying about what your mother thinks. *She* married who she wanted to marry … pfft! And God help anyone who might've stood in her way!' He chuckles. 'This is *your* life. Only you know what you truly want.'

'But … but I don't want to hurt anyone.'

Dad takes off his specs and rubs his forehead thoughtfully. 'Listen, love, no matter what you do, somebody's heart's going to wind up broken. Just make sure it's not yours.'

*****

'Merry Christmas, honey,' Brian chirps, handing me a small, posh-looking white giftbag in the sitting room after breakfast.

I go on to feign excitement at unboxing a gold Rolex watch which would look far more at home on Mother's snobby little wrist than mine. It's not that I'm ungrateful, it's just not very *me* and I can't help but feel nauseous at the cost of what I deem to be a massive, ugly watch – particularly when the world is rife with poverty. It's a drop in the ocean to someone like Brian who will never live off fifteen pence noodles in the long run up to payday, but something way less expensive would have functioned just as well. Although, the function of a Rolex watch, I suspect, is more about displaying one's financial status rather than the actual time.

What I hand over to Brian in return is by no means on the same level. I mean, what do you gift someone who already has everything they ever wanted? Socks, obviously. I mean, normal, tasteful socks. He barely reacts as he opens them. In fact, I think I detect a slight wave of disappointment at the lack of bold stripes or loud patterns that scream 'I'm trying to be cool and fun'.

My face falls as Mother unboxes a Rolex watch of her very own from Brian, prompting a symphony of long gasps and unpleasant squealing sounds.

'Oh, Brian, you shouldn't have! You really shouldn't have!' she bawls, ripping it from the box and quickly replacing the existing one on her wrist – the one Dad got her for their silver wedding anniversary – with it.

Dad also unboxes a Rolex watch, shooting me a look that says 'Oh, fuck! Isn't this awkward? Do we hand them back if and when you give him the boot?'.

I take myself off to the shower where, other than for when I'm lying awake at night with my mind working overtime while the street sleeps on, I get to think. I still haven't come up with anything verging at all close to a decision. I guess, like Dad says, I need to accept that someone's going to wind up hurt in all this, only I'd sooner it was me than anyone else. I've dealt with rejection all my life. I'm used to it. I guess that's the problem – I know how it feels and I wouldn't wish it on anyone, particularly good souls like Brian and Dan.

I decide to pop my dilemma into a mental cardboard box and shelve it at the back of my mind so I can get through Christmas with my sanity intact, although I'm fully aware it will fall off said shelf with a loud thud, the contents spilling out to the forefront of my mind every now and then. When New Year hits, I should be better primed for new beginnings and armed with that sudden, immense motivation the 1st January seems to trigger in us all.

Later, while stationed on the sofa watching classic British Christmas television – and able to actually hear it with Mother and her shrill voice tucked away in the kitchen preparing lunch – an excited Brian bustles in through the sitting room door wearing a snowman-patterned tie that I didn't even know he owned.

'Hey, honey! Look! I got your phone working again!' he announces, brandishing it in his hand victoriously.

My face falls in horror. Not just at the crap tie, but at the prospect of any number of texts from "Sexy Pants" pinging through at any given moment. Consequently, I spring up from the sofa and snatch it from him in a vicious seagull-like manner.

'Oh, er ... sorry, I'm just thrilled you got it working!' I blag, putting on a fake smile and flushing a little pink. 'How did you manage it?'

'It was the rice trick,' he replies, slightly miffed.

'Amazing!' I praise, giving him an appreciative hug before hurriedly announcing I need the loo and leaving him standing staring numbly at *Chitty Chitty Bang Bang* on the TV.

I dart upstairs to stick the other SIM card back in it before the inevitable happens. I breathe a sigh of relief as it slots back in with minimal sweary fuss and the Dan-SIM finds its way back into the hidden depths of the Kate Spade bag. Yuletide can now proceed without the looming threat of illicit revelations spilling out dramatically over Christmas dinner in the manner of some cliché soap opera ... Phew!

'Elizabeth! Button up your trousers and sit up at once! The Queen's speech is coming on any second, and I will *not* have you lying about in that manner when the Queen is on the television,' Mother demands, breezing into the sitting room after dinner to find me sprawled on the sofa with my flies undone.

'I think she enjoyed a little too much of that pavlova of yours,' Brian smirks, patting my belly in a slightly patronising tone.

He's not wrong. I've enjoyed a little too much – well, a fucking lot – of everything since I got here, such that I can literally feel my waistline expanding to the next dress size by the second. Oh, well, it's Christmas! If you can't enjoy yourself at Christmas, when the hell can you? I'll get back on the dormouse diet in plenty of time before the wedding ... Not that I'm even certain there'll *be* one.

*****

As ever, making us all question the long and drawn out build up for one day which essentially passes in a boozy, gluttonous blur, the madness and mayhem of Christmas is done and dusted for another year. I wonder where I'll be by the time the next comes around. Married to Brian, or to Mr Wonderful?

Lying wide awake during what are the small hours of New Year's Eve morning, I quietly anticipate the imminent surge of motivation that is bound to hit soon and help me out of this big bastard of a dilemma.

With Brian snoring on beside me, my heart quietly breaks as I come to terms with the fact that it's Dan I truly want. Something I guess I always knew but haven't gone as far as to fully admit out loud ... well, mentally out loud.

I've got it all planned out:

> 1. Will meet with Dan at his place before I leave UK to let him know I accept his proposal. Will try upmost to resist shagging arse off him during said meeting until

have done right by Brian.

2. Will fly back to US with Brian and gently break it to him while in his eight-bedroomed comfort zone.

3. Brian will take rebuttal in calm, Buddha-like manner and remain in cheerful disposition while I clear eight-bedroomed comfort zone of my possessions.

4. Will hand back fuck-off great engagement ring and massive Rolex.

5. Will have Brooke busy cancelling wedding plans in background, organising non-refundable goods to be sold and proceeds gifted to charity.

6. Brooke will buy my share of business, leaving extra funds for Dan and I to marry and set up home together.

7. Will flee back to UK on earliest flight possible to be with Mr Wonderful and avoid wrath of Duchess.

8. Will visit parents with Dan by my side to break news after having shagged arse off him with lights fully on now body in way better nick.

9. Mother will accept everything with little fuss.

10. Marry Mr Wonderful, become Mrs Elliott and live out rest of days in wedded bliss.

Sounds like a plan!

*****

Next morning, Mother bursts into the kitchen while I'm mid-swig of the orange juice I'm drinking straight from the carton, causing it to spill down my front as she scares the shit out of me with that bloody voice.

'Oh, don't do that dear, it's most unhygienic!'

I turn to face her, open-mouthed.

'Good grief, look at the state of you!' she barks. 'I do hope you'll be smartening up! You can't skulk about in a state of decay on New Year's Eve, dear.'

'It's only 8.30am, Mother! I don't know anyone who'd be done up to the nines at this time of the day other than for you ... *and* Duchess,' I scoff, slamming the fridge door.

'Hm, which reminds me I must find out what colour that woman will be wearing to the wedding,' Mother muses as she sets about shining the hob with brute force. 'I will not have her slinking around in my cornflower blue!'

Just as I'm wrapping up the transformation from state of decay to state of wahey, I frown at the sight of my reflection in the mirrored door of the wardrobe, appalled at the belly straining within my tailored black shift dress. Oh, for God's sake, I thought *you'd* fucked off for good!

Brian emerges from the en suite bathroom draped in a towel, his eyes immediately coming to rest on my middle.

Existence of Mr Greedy belly confirmed by second party! Oh, fuck!

'Is there something you wanna tell me?' he chuckles, raising a brow suggestively.

Funnily enough, yes, but that's not for now. Er, hang on a bloody minute, did he just commit the cardinal sin of alluding to my looking pregnant when I'm nothing of the sort?! Yes, he *did* ... Bastard!

'Thanks a lot!' I huff, although on further inspection he has a point. I do actually look pregnant.

'You're not, are you?' he probes dangerously.

I spin around in readiness to tear a strip off him as the realisation dawns that I can't remember when I was last inconvenienced with my period. Seems like ages ago. Definitely longer than a month. No. Shut up. I can't be ... Can I?

I stand staring at him, speechless. My mouth hangs open and my face twitches as I try to process everything from the prospect of being with child when, in my mind, I'm still a child myself, to my immense feelings for Dan and the fact that if am indeed pregnant with Brian, I will definitely not be enjoying adventurous lights-on sex with Dan, nor taking his surname anytime soon. Or indeed, in this lifetime.

'Lizzie, say something,' Brian urges, looking anxious.

'I-I don't know,' I stammer, going stiff.

'Well then, I think we'd better get a cab into town and go get a test,' he chirps, an excited grin creeping up his face while the frown lines on mine deepen.

Chapter 3:

Goodbye Butterflies

'Please be negative. Please be negative. Please be negative. Please be negative,' I chant in a whisper under my breath, gripping the sink for support as the pregnancy test develops on the vanity unit to my side.

'How's it going?' Brian calls from outside the door of the en suite.

'Er, just a minute,' I call back to him, heart pounding and knees trembling in trepidation.

I've never been the maternal type, but the prospect of starting a family with Dan had always featured somewhere within the many daydreams I've had about him. Now, as I stand here faced with the prospect of achieving such milestones with somebody else, I can't help but feel an enormous sense of regret. Not at the life that may or may not be growing inside of me, but for the missed chance to have the fairy tale, my happy ever after, with the man I love. I love

Brian, but I'm not *in* love with him the way I am with Dan. It's taken me all this time to learn the difference.

Taking a deep breath and hoping and praying with every fibre of my being for a negative result, I flip the test over and take a moment to process the lines that read like a life sentence to me.

Positive.

I'm having Brian's baby.

I burst into tears and sink to my knees, swathed in guilt for the sense of grief I'm feeling. It's as though the butterflies I've been carrying for Dan in my stomach this whole time just died on me all at once. Well, that's it then. I guess the future's decided, and that decision has been taken out of my hands.

A minute or so later, I open the bathroom door a panda-eyed snivelling mess.

Brian's face falls. 'It's negative?'

'No, positive,' I tell him, holding up the test.

'Oh jeez! You're kidding me?! Well, that's great! This is amazing!' he gasps, punching the air. 'Holy moly! I'm gonna be a dad!'

Observing I'm not expressing the same level of excitement, Brian's ecstatic grin dampens somewhat. 'Don't worry, honey, I'm sure they can do something with the wedding dress. Or we'll get you another, anything you like, whatever the cost!'

I nod in agreement, pretending that's all it is – as though I'm the type of person for whom it's the end of the world when faced with the prospect of not looking the dog's bollocks in a couture gown.

'Listen, I love you and you've made me the happiest man alive!' Brian grins, patting my belly affectionately. 'And with this little one in tow, we really are the dream team!'

I nod, tasking every facial muscle I possess to force a smile.

*****

'Okay, everybody, if I could grab your attention for just a moment,' Brian announces, slinking in through the sitting room door a little before midnight holding a tray of four champagne glasses: three containing champagne, one orange juice.

Mother and Dad glance up from the sofa pre-emptively while my heart sinks a little deeper into what is surely now sub-zero depths of despair. He's not going to tell them, is he? I'd quietly assumed we wouldn't be telling anyone until I'd had it confirmed and passed the three-month mark – that's what most people do, right?

'Well, firstly, I'd like to thank you guys for being

such wonderful hosts. You've made me so welcome in your home and, oh boy, I have to say Christmas lunch was the best I've tasted yet, Petunia,' Brian gushes.

'Oh, Brian! And to think of all the restaurants you must've eaten at in your time!' Mother gasps, patting down her hair with a triumphant smirk and basking in the praise.

'And dare I say it,' he adds, continuing on with the charm offensive, 'it was even better than Mom's!' He grins, instantly scoring himself a million brownie points as Mother squeals with joy at getting one up on Duchess.

'So, next year is already fixed to be some year what with the wedding happening,' Brian goes on.

Mother gives a slow, firm nod.

Dad glances at me shadily then quickly looks away.

'But it just got a whole lot better!' he announces, pausing and looking at me as though he might burst with pride at any moment. 'Because ... you guys are going to be grandparents!'

What is quite possibly the most unpleasant, highly-pitched, deafening sound to come from Mother yet rings through the air in response to the news. It's a noise I imagine lottery winners make once they've matched the last of the winning numbers, safe in the knowledge that whatever the neighbours think is no longer a concern now that they'll be living in grass skirts in paradise.

In the moments that follow as midnight strikes and Big Ben dongs, I finally dare to look Dad's way. He doesn't have to say anything out loud as the look he gives me confirms what I already know. Dan Elliott is history.

*****

I've barely slept, my mind a non-stop conveyor belt of thoughts as Brian sleeps on soundly beside me. There's something I still need to do and I'm dreading it.

'Would you drive me to Dan's?' I ask Dad discreetly in the kitchen next morning.

'Are you sure that's a good idea?' he mutters back wide-eyed, cautiously peering over his shoulder.

'I need to tell him where he stands,' I plead.

With Brian busy undertaking his morning shower ritual and Mother's focus on packing away the plethora of pricey intricate baubles from the Christmas tree, it's possibly the only opportunity I'm going to get before Brian and I fly back to the US tomorrow. Turning down a marriage proposal isn't something to be done by telephone – I mean, you'd have to be a pretty cold-hearted bitch.

'Okay, love. I'll tell your mother we're popping out to the shop,' he says, strolling off to fetch his car keys.

'So, when exactly did you find out you were expecting?' Dad quizzes me during the drive to Dan's.

'Only yesterday,' I reply, picking at my lifting gel nail polish glumly.

'And do you want this baby?' he asks, turning his head to look at me briefly with a grave expression.

'It's not that I don't want the baby, it's more that I don't want Brian,' I reply, my eyes welling.

Dad nods. 'Well, it's certainly a spanner in the works, but…' he muses, trailing off.

'What?' I ask, turning to look at him.

He clears his throat. 'Well, there are still options available.'

'N-no. Oh, no!' I tell him, my voice wobbling. 'Sometimes it's the right thing for other women, but, well, there are women out there in far worse situations. Brian loves me, he's on cloud bloody nine. This baby will want for nothing. Even if I could look past all that and go on to find all the happiness in the world with Dan after, I … well

'... it would always be there at the back of my mind.'

'I know, love, really, I do. But it's a double-sided coin. You've also got to ask yourself whether it's the right thing to add a child to all of this. It won't last you know, you and Brian. You can't go on living a lie.'

I say nothing as we turn into Dan's street, my heart quickening as I spot his car from a mile away.

'Look, love, you can't confine yourself to a life of misery to keep others happy,' Dad sighs, pulling into a space and turning to face me.

'Are *you* blissfully happy with Mother?' I challenge him, causing him to go all stiff.

'Well, er ... er... This isn't about me,' he stumbles awkwardly, his expression doing all the talking.

'Then it *is* possible to live a lie, Dad. You're doing it yourself,' I point out, raising my brows.

'I suppose you're right, love.' He sighs. 'If only we both had an ounce of your mother's nerve!'

I leave Dad despondently scanning his newspaper as I attempt to exit the car with my seat belt on, causing him, myself, and the car to lurch violently.

Ugh, let's try that again, shall we?

Shakily, I make my way up the steps to the main door and ring the buzzer to Dan's apartment, standing back in anticipation.

'Hello?' comes his oh-so-dreamy chocolate voice.

'H-hi Lan, it's Dizzie,' I blurt out.

Shit, I can't even talk properly!

He laughs. 'Dizzie?!'

'Ugh, I mean Lizzie. It's Lizzie,' I correct myself, turning pink and thanking the heavens he can't see me through this intercom.

'Come on up!'

I stand in angst outside his door, dying inside for the millionth time over as he opens it back looking thrilled to see me, as well as devastatingly handsome. His dashing smile soon drops as I burst into tears.

'What is it, Lizzie? What's wrong?' he asks, taking my hand and leading me inside, flinging the door shut behind me.

'I-I can't marry you,' I tell him, observing his face crumple. 'I just found out I'm p-pregnant. I'm having Brian's baby.'

Dan says nothing. He just stands looking back at me, the pain in his eyes clearly visible.

'I h-had it all planned,' I continue in between a series of sobs. 'I was g-going to come here to accept your proposal, then fly back to the US with Brian and tell him everything there, cancel the wedding and make arrangements to move back here to be with y-you. But then ... then this,' I tell him, gesturing toward my belly.

'How does he feel about it? Brian, I mean,' Dan asks despondently, looking down at my middle too.

'He's over the m-moon, couldn't be h-happier,' I sob.

Dan nods empathetically. 'And what about you?'

'I've g-got to have this baby,' I concede. 'I'm staying with Brian.'

A long silence follows, which Dan eventually breaks. 'But, if you were planning to leave him, you're not going to be happy, surely?'

'It's not about me now. The baby's the priority. It changes everything,' I reason.

'Well ... Well, what if we bring the baby up together?' Dan suggests, eyes darting in desperation.

He would do that? Bring up another man's child just to be with me? Ugh, my heart!

'Oh, Dan, it would be so easy if Brian was a bastard.' I sigh. 'But he's ... he's a good man and he's so excited about becoming a dad. I can't take his child away from him. It's not like we'd be just down the road – we'd be five thousand miles away in a different country. I could never do that to him.'

Dan nods, clearly unable to contest the logic.

'So, you see I have no choice, Dan. I'm sorry. I wish things were different but…' I trail off as my throat starts closing up on me.

'I understand,' he says finally. He bites his lip, his gaze firmly fixed at his feet.

'It's for the best. This is how it's got to be,' I say resolutely, trying not to observe the guns folded out in front of him. 'I best be getting back. I haven't got long.'

His arms fall to his sides. 'Look, I wish you guys all the best. I really hope everything goes well with the baby,' he says, not even the slightest hint of resentment in his tone. Just heartache. A whole lot of heartache.

'Thank you. Take care, Dan,' I whisper, unable to catch my breath as emotion takes over.

'You too, Lizzie.'

So, this is it. The last goodbye. We stand, gazing at one another until, with the greatest reluctance, I turn to leave, not quite able to say it.

'Oh, love,' Dad soothes sympathetically as I clamber back into the car a sobbing wreck. He pulls me into a firm side hug and we sit for a bit while I cry my heart out, making the car shake all over again.

*****

'Take care of that grandchild of mine!' Mother roars, her voice echoing loudly through the airport. 'Don't you be pumping him full of potato crisps!'

Him?

'Oh, she won't. Only good, nutritious food from hereon in, right, honey?' Brian nods toward me as we stand before departures, bound for New York.

Yeah, good luck with that!

'Hmmm,' I mumble quietly, considering my options for bakeries and sweet shops within walking distance of the office.

'Cheerio, love,' Dad squeaks, patting my back. 'Proud of you,' he murmurs discreetly into my hair.

I nod, pressing my lips together to steady the wobble. 'Bye, Dad.'

As we taxi along the runway, there's still a part of me that wants to tear off my seatbelt and bang down the cockpit door, demanding the captain stop the plane at once on account of the torturous imagery playing on my mind of Dan moving on at some point with another woman. I cannot *stand* the thought of him with another woman! Disney-prince-kissing her! Giving her sports massages! Drinking her up in hot tubs! Giving her multiple orgasms ... my multiple orgasms! Furthermore, if he deems her to be right person – 2.0 – he'll propose to her with his nan's ring ... my ring! My precious! Ugh, what a shit-kicking life.

I sit with narrowed eyes as my voice of reason slaps down the spoilt brat in me.

Oh, pull yourself together! You've no right whingeing, I mean, really! There are people out there with far worse problems. You've an eight-bedroomed roof over your head, a successful business, a good man who loves you, a baby on the way and...

Sigh.

I drown in a multitude of emotions as we take off. With every passing second, I seem to launch from melancholy to guilt, grief, jealousy, and then extreme rage. This could get dangerous. All Brian has to do is breathe the wrong way and he very well may be in for a Chinese burn!

Later, back on American soil...

'So, I called Mom to tell her the good news!' Brian announces, strolling into the bedroom in pants that really do him no favours where sexual appeal is concerned.

I lay in a jetlagged heap in bed, staring up at the ceiling. Oh, for fuck's sake. If it wasn't bad enough that he practically went and spilled his guts before I'd even pulled up my knickers post-pregnancy test, *now* he's gone and blabbed to Duchess!

'But shouldn't we really wait before we announce it to the world? At least until I'm past the three-month mark,' I reason.

'Well, *your* folks know, so it seemed unfair that Mom was in the dark about it,' he coolly counters. 'We're hardly telling the world.'

Yes, but *she* bloody will. And my folks only know because *he* couldn't wait to tell them.

'Besides,' he adds, selecting a crisply folded set of pyjamas from the chest of drawers, 'you're looking like you're already past the three-month mark anyway. More like five, I would guess.'

My mouth hangs open in dismay. Did he really just say that? Bastard! I am not five months gone!

'You think I'm daft enough not to question five months without a bloody period?' I argue.

He raises a brow suggestively, saying nothing.

'You do, don't you?!' I explode, my head wobbling in outrage.

'Whoa! What's the matter with you? You've

been so uptight ever since we got back,' he remarks, holding his hands up defensively.

'I was perfectly fine until you pretty much told the *New York Post* we're expecting, then went on to fat shame me!' I protest.

He stares back at me, dumbfounded. 'Look, I'm not going to get into an argument. I know it's just the pregnancy hormones, probably made worse by the jet lag, so I'll let you off.' He chuckles, catapulting my rage to a whole new level.

'Right! Right! Well, you've done it now,' I mutter, flinging back the bedcovers and darting out the bed.

'Ugh, Lizzie, what are you doing?' he groans, daring to roll his eyes at me.

'I'm going to sleep in the farthest away room from *you*, you great ... tosser!' I shout, noticing his look of confusion at what is a very British insult. Probably for the best. I don't want to fight with him, really, I don't, but someone's got to get it today and ... well, he ought to bloody well choose his words more carefully.

It seems to me that whenever Brian's in the company of, or had contact with, Duchess, he turns into an arse. A strange phenomenon I duly brand "the Duch-ass effect". Playing the part of the mature, responsible adult, Brian turns his back to me as though dealing with a toddler mid-tantrum, even though *he* essentially pissed the toddler off and caused the bloody tantrum.

Even as I stomp defiantly out the bedroom I know I'm behaving like a child, but the audible tut just as I'm half out the door serves as a red rag to a bull such that I quickly find myself excelling to massive twat territory as I proceed to wiggle off my engagement ring and throw it over my shoulder in the hallway, hearing a metallic *ding* as it bounces off the marble flooring. Ugh! What did I do that for? I'm not sure, but it felt like a good alternative means of stress relief versus beating Brian about the head with one of those stupid bloody slippers!

I skulk into one of the many bedrooms wastefully surplus to Brian's needs where I lie in bed stewing, Dad's words about Brian and I not lasting echoing through my mind. Not lasting isn't an option. We've got to make things work for the baby's sake; with or without the third member of our marriage – as in Duchess, not Dan Elliott, sadly. I've got to face up to my responsibilities. It takes two to tango, even if my only part in the conception was lying there like a bit of wet rag. The baby didn't ask to be conceived, did it? Hmm, yes. It's time to accept things as they are. To step up to the plate. I've got to take my focus off Mr Wonderful and apply it to what is soon to be my own little family.

Stroking my belly, I begin picturing the baby; what he or she might look like and the little personality they'll go on to develop. I can't at all imagine how the immensely houseproud Brian is going to cope with all the broken ornaments, upturned plants and doodling on the walls once they start toddling. I let out a vengeful snigger as I picture him running about like a blue-arsed fly in those bloody moccasins, frantically trying to clear up the trail of destruction one-handedly, mid-business call.

As I lie here alone for once without Brian or anyone else fussing and getting on my tits, I feel a sudden sense of unconditional love for this tiny bean – or watermelon, as Brian would have me think. A chance to pause for thought and consider the miracle happening inside of me, a miracle some poor women are cruelly denied by Mother Nature for one reason or another.

Eyes growing heavy, I succumb to sleep, partly pissed off and partly counting my blessings.

*****

'When was your last period?' Brian's doctor asks as I sit before him nervously the next morning.

Ah, the million-dollar question! My gormless expression tells him I haven't the foggiest.

'Don't you track your cycle dates in a diary or something?' Brian asks, sat at my side but still very much in the doghouse. Well, perhaps half in, half out since he did bring me breakfast in bed this morning, although he lost a few brownie points along the way whingeing about crumbs in the bed.

Come on now, Brian. Do you really think I'm that efficient? Anyway, hold up a second, why would anyone not trying to conceive waste time they'll never get back tracking the most unpleasant time of the month? Pfft! Men!

'Er, no,' I reply, shooting Mr Efficient a warning look that says 'Mention "five months" again and you shall be dealt with!'.

'That's okay, the scan will tell us for certain,' Doc murmurs, tap-tapping away on his computer.

'So, how soon can we have the scan?' Brian asks, looking hopeful.

'This afternoon, if that's not too early?'

'This afternoon's perfect,' he chirps, his face lighting up just as his phone rings for the umpteenth time this morning. He rushes to answer before, God forbid, the company is plunged into wrack and ruin at the hands of the many top business professionals paid mega bucks to help run it.

Well, at least now Brian will soon be able to see for himself that I am nowhere near five bloody months gone, cheeky bastard! Ugh. Really must stop dwelling.

'Okay, this is going to feel a little cold,' the sonographer warns, squirting a massive dollop of freezing cold gel onto my lower stomach, the bottle making a loud *parp*. She proceeds to yank back the waistband of my leggings and undies, forcibly tucking a paper towel over the top of them and practically fully exposing my special area in the process. Alright, love, calm down! I know *you've* seen it all before, but *mine* happens to be the lesser-spotted foof! Jeez, I've heard nothing's sacred when you're having a baby, but Christ, let mine develop first before we start with all that.

'Okay, let's meet baby!' She grins with slightly mad eyes, plonking herself down in the seat beside the scan equipment as Brian and I exchange nervous-excited glances.

She sweeps the probe across my belly and we sit frowning at the strange distorted moving shapes on the screen, with not the slightest clue as to what we're looking at.

'Is that it there to the left, or just a lump of womb?' I ask brusquely.

Brian raises a brow as if to imply he can't take me anywhere. To be fair, he can't. Here we are at a pricey, private clinic and I'm showing us up already.

'Ah, here we are!' she announces, perfectly ignoring me as she homes in on what appears to be a little pulsating blob. 'Here's baby.'

'Wow!' Brian gasps, reaching for my hand as we both tear up.

Wow, indeed! A couple of blue stripes on a pregnancy test doesn't drive the message home that there's a little person cooking away inside of you in quite the same way a scan does. All of a sudden, it seems to really hit home. Am I worried about being responsible for a helpless infant? Who, me? Me, who can't follow instructions as simple as the "cut here" line displayed on resealable cheese packaging, cutting anywhere but and instantly rendering it un-re-sealable and bringing about its rapid demise? Me, who doesn't realise my top has been inside out all day until I go to take it off at night, spot the label on the outside, then begin a frantic mental assessment of the day and all the people who saw me and it? Me, who arrives home to find my car stolen and rushes to call the police before realising I drove to work and took the bus home while away with the fairies? Nah, not worried in the slightest.

'So, er, how far along in the pregnancy would you say I am?' I ask the sonographer, giving Brian a sideways glance.

She clicks her tongue and makes a calculative sound, studying the data on the screen closely.

'You look to be measuring around ten weeks,'

she says, immediately proving me right and Brian deliciously wrong.

Feeling smug, I shoot him a look that silently screams 'Ha! Told yer!', but am quickly appalled at realising the Mr Greedy belly I've amassed is probably three parts gluttony, one part baby.

Later, the sonographer hands us a photo of the scan during my struggle to haul myself off the bed. Slipping one hand into Brian's, I pull the wedgie of my dental floss lace underwear – now much tighter than I remember – out of my crack with the other and we leave the clinic on an amazing high, despite the whirlwind of emotions of the past few weeks. I get to thinking that if merely seeing our baby this afternoon has brought us this much closer this quickly, then just imagine how we'll be as a family unit when he or she arrives.

It's said that the happiest people in life don't have the best of everything, they *make* the best of everything. I'm sure that, in time, Brian and I can go the distance, I tell myself as we walk to the car. All I have to do is rediscover the feelings I had for him at the start of our relationship. Shouldn't be too hard, should it?

Mere seconds later, the only thing I go on to rediscover about Brian is my pet bloody peeve when he suddenly exclaims, 'Ooh, honey, almost forgot, Mom's coming over for dinner tonight,' whistling casually as we enter the car.

The future mother-in-law dropping by for dinner practically unannounced is probably no biggie to most, but since we are talking about Duchess, I respond by slamming the door aggressively and scowl out the passenger window for the journey. To anyone watching from outside, I must look a picture as my angry wasp face whizzes past!

We stop by the grocery store on the way home. Brian's a bloody nightmare to go shopping with. Always so stressy and tense, on constant alert to his phone ringing. It's as though any non-business task in his life is done at break-neck speed with the purpose of freeing up more hours in the day for business. He grabs a trolley and he's off, whizzing through the aisles like Mo Farah after twenty Red Bulls.

Five minutes into our shopping trip and I've lost him already. Ugh! I hate it when he fucks off with the trolley, leaving me to struggle around the store with my arms full, frantically scanning every aisle for him.

Eventually, I spot him down the health food aisle browsing manuka honey, the knob! With a face like a displeased cod, arms killing me from my candy aisle grab, I stride toward him and drop my sugary stash aggressively into the trolley.

'Now don't even start!' I warn. 'I'm craving shit and if I want to eat shit, I'll eat shit, okay?!'

He turns around to face me, prompting my entire body to seize up as I observe it's not even him. Instead, it's some guy with an uncannily Brian-like back of head wearing an equally Brian-like white shirt.

I close my eyes in humiliation, turning scarlet as I proceed to furiously fetch out the shit tonne of crap I just dumped in his trolley.

'Sorry, sorry!' I mumble. 'I er ... thought you were my fiancé.'

'No problem.' He coughs awkwardly, the pair of us cringing during the lengthening silence that follows as I scrabble about, rummaging through his much healthier goods for my items, my mind awhirl with visions of strangling Brian the second I get my hands on him!

Note to self: Might be good idea to identify "Jetpack Brian" by his actual face during future aisle scans going forward.

Chapter 4:

Apron Strings

'Hello again, Lizzie,' Duchess greets me in a slow, monotone voice as she saunters in through the front door, air kissing both sides of my face.

Hey, biatch!

'Oh, hello, Veronica,' I coo, my voice raising an octave from the fakery.

'And how have we been keeping?' she enquires, more as a challenge than concern for my welfare a she eyes the front of my hoodie contemptuously.

I peer down at it, noticing slobbish stains from various foodstuffs I totally didn't know I was sporting. Bugger.

'Good, thank you,' I reply, trying not to choke on the fumes of her perfume. Fuck me, she must be 100% proof! Nobody had better light a match! 'And you?' I quickly add, forcing a smile.

'Mm, yes, very well,' she mumbles, forcing one

of her own.

Duchess pats her hair and then looks at mine. I reach my hand up to my head, trying to make it seem nonchalant. Damn! I had attempted to tidy myself up for Duchess's looming visit, but it looks like my bastard hair isn't playing ball. It's as though it deliberately sets out to conform for days on end when sat about doing fuck-all so that I develop a sense of trust in it. Then, the minute I need to look a bit presentable for an impending visit from scary future mother-in-law, a ringleader hair jumps up and yells 'Ah! I feel a protest coming on! Who shall we impersonate this time my fellow strands? Einstein? Nah, we do him quite a bit. How about Russell Brand, then? No, better still, Boris Johnson!'.

Ugh. It seems to be thinning out on the lengths and ends yet is mad and bird's nest-like at the roots. I did attempt to tie it back, but it only looked even worse. All I need are two tight rollers for each side of my head and I'd have been fucking Mozart! I mean, what do you do with hair like that, save for shaving the bastard off?

'Hello, soldier, how did the scan go?' Duchess asks Brian as soon as he walks into the hallway, as though it was him who'd had it.

'Hey, Duch. Oh, great! Baby's doing just fine. He's measuring in at 10-11 weeks,' he replies, grinning from ear to ear.

He? Why does everyone insist on referring to the baby as a boy? It seems to be a foregone conclusion that I'm growing a Brian Jr when it could very well be a mini-me! Hmph, wishful thinking probably, because if I *am* carrying a girl then God help Brian and his posh, organic cotton bath towels, the volume of which is destined to double due to destruction by fake tan!

Duchess eyes me over dinner like a lioness sizing up her prey.

'Well, you certainly look bigger than ten weeks,' she remarks. 'I don't know, so many women take the term "eating for two" literally these days.' She laughs pompously.

Wow! Now I totally get why Brian has zero understanding of tact.

'Well, I've been eating for four,' I announce, cool as you like, not even looking up from my plate.

I sense her prolonged glare boring into me as the butler arrives at the table and mumbles something unintelligible in Brian's ear. I freeze as he holds out my engagement ring in his hand. Ah, fuck! I'd quite forgotten all about throwing it in a strop last night.

'Lizzie? The cleaner found your ring on the floor upstairs,' Brian announces, looking surprised.

'Oh. It probably slipped off,' I gabble, staring intently at my peas as though they were the most fascinating things in the world.

'I didn't realise it was loose?' he probes.

'Hmm, if anything it should be tighter,' Duchess remarks, eyeing me suspiciously under overdrawn brows.

'Well, yes, it was feeling a bit tight so I took it off and I must've dropped it,' I reason, feeling an overwhelming urge to grab Duchess's seabass by the tail and bash it about that pestiferous face of hers.

She turns to me and lowers her voice discreetly. 'You could buy a house for the price of that ring, perhaps you ought to be a bit more careful with it,' she hisses.

Ignoring her, I take the ring from Brian and slip it back on my finger, feeling terrible for having thrown it but also kind of within my rights ... particularly when Brian launches into full Duch-ass mode: How's your food, Duch? More wine, Duch? Are you warm enough, Duch? Can I get you anything else, Duch? Am I still the best son ever, Duch?

Sigh.

As we get onto dessert, Duchess turns to face me.

'I thought I might come along to your wedding

dress fitting at the weekend,' she announces, instantly causing the hairs on the back of my neck to stand to attention.

'Yeah, wouldn't that be great? You girls together!' Brian chirps.

No, it wouldn't be, Brian. It absolutely bloody well wouldn't be.

'Oh, I-I,' I stutter, my mind going ten to the dozen trying to think of excuses as to why she can't.

'Of course, you'll be stuck for things to do now with all the spare time you're going to have. So, we can perhaps get together more often,' she butts in with an alligator-like grin.

'Spare time?' I repeat, confused.

'Yes, well, you'll be jacking in that business of yours, surely?'

I frown, sensing impending conflict. 'Why would I do that?'

She stares at me for a few moments with a dumbfounded expression. 'Well, why would you tire yourself working when Brian is as wealthy as he is? It's not as if you need what little money you make from it, is it? Besides, a wife's place is in the home.'

I look in Brian's direction but he says nothing – as ever. It's all I can do not to spring up out of my chair like the Incredible Hulk, tear my hoodie to pieces, grab and lift Duchess high over my head and throw her across the room. In reality, I simply take a deep breath, just about managing to keep my shit together and calmly state my case.

'It's not about the money, Veronica,' I explain in a calm voice. 'Working gives me a sense of pride and independence. I love what I do and I've no plans to "jack it in" anytime soon,' I add, amazed at having retained such poise.

She laughs mockingly. 'But you're about to become a mother! What are you planning to do, palm the baby off onto some nanny while you play at being entrepreneurs with that silly ex-roommate of yours?'

Don't bite, Lizzie! Don't bite! Er, *no*, actually! Why should I sit here being all calm and respectful when *she* can sit churning out insult after insult, unchallenged?

'Actually, that silly ex-roommate of mine is a shit-hot businesswoman!' I protest, spraying the table with tiramisu. 'She's making good money, supporting herself and paying into the system, like most women have been doing since the Dark Ages. There's more to life than keeping house and popping babies out your arse, you know!'

Duchess sneers at me in contempt, her face like a vexed camel. Brian gulps in horror.

'Do excuse me, I've come over all nauseous,' I announce, rising from my seat and striding out of the room toward the kitchen where I rake through the cupboards in search of my sweet stash, leaving Brian's orderly-fashioned tins and foodstuffs in a state of disarray.

Mental note: Think I left bag of Haribo Tangfastics in stranger's trolley earlier. Bugger! Really fancied a fizzy croc.

Like a wary munchkin, I come out of hiding once the Wicked Witch of the West has left.

'Your Mum hates me,' I complain to Brian, shuffling out from the cloakroom bathroom toward the staircase.

'Get outta town! She doesn't hate …' he begins, trailing off in surprise as he turns to observe my trousers hanging halfway down to my knees.

'Lizzie, why are your pants like that?' he asks, pointing to my legs.

'Oh, well there's no point going to all the trouble of pulling them up when I'm only going to take them off for bed in a second,' I reason, staring at him as though he missed a trick.

Before he can answer, the butler walks in and almost falls over in shock. Fuck! What's *he* still doing here? I thought he was long gone! I move to yank up my trousers again quicker than I've ever moved before in my life.

'Pardon me, sir, will you be needing anything

else before I leave for the evening?' he asks Brian.

To un-see what he just saw would be fucking marvellous!

'Er, no, thank you,' Brian tells him, looking mortified.

Wow! A perfectly fitting ending to a crap day.

To-do list:

1. Show hair who's boss
2. Show Brian who's boss (i.e. not bloody Duchess)
3. Replace perineum-torturing underwear with selection of large, comfy pants
4. Purchase several bags Haribo Tangfastics

*****

'Oh-em-gee, I've missed your face so much!' Brooke screams, rushing toward me as I plod in through the door at work the next Monday.

'Ditto!' I pant as she grabs and half squeezes me to death.

'I've had nobody to laugh at! It's been so

shit!' she yells, almost deafening me. 'Whoah! What the fuck?!' she gasps as I take off my coat. 'You're ... You're ...'

'Yes, I am!' I smile timidly.

'It's Dan's, isn't it?! You gave in and screwed him, didn't you?!' she accuses, looking horrified.

'No, it's not bloody Dan's. I've only been away a few weeks! I'm ten weeks gone. Last time Dan entered me was nearly two years ago,' I recall sadly.

'So, it's Brian's then?'

'Yes, of course it's Brian's,' I groan.

'Right, I'm gonna make us both a latte and you're gonna tell me everything there is to know,' Brooke instructs, hurrying off through the back door to the kitchen area.

'Good call!' I agree, what with Brian having banned me from drinking coffee at home because it's 'not good for the baby'.

Over the course of the next twenty minutes, I pour my heart out, interrupted by the phone a few times. Ugh! Where do these sickeningly loved-up couples get off?

Having gotten the full low-down, Brooke sits in a despondent silence, staring at the floor.

'Look, my head's in a better place about it all now, honestly. Don't worry about me, I'll be fine,' I tell her.

'Oh, I wasn't,' she replies matter-of-factly, 'I was just thinking what a terrible waste of fine cock ... Dan, I mean.'

My mouth falls open, but she's right.

'Well, how do you think I feel?! I had to reject it in favour of spending the rest of my life staring at the ceiling while Brian has his once-weekly missionary grind on me.'

'Is it that bad?' Brooke probes.

'It's even worse than usual now because he's being "gentle" so as not to hurt the baby,' I complain.

'Gentle as in crap?'

'Hm, exactly!' I agree, glancing at my phone to make sure it hasn't somehow called Brian while I sit slagging him off in the worst possible way. 'But to be perfectly honest, it's actually a relief not having to put out as often,' I add, rolling my eyes.

'God, girl, you sound like a menopausal housewife and you've not even married the guy yet. Not good!' Brooke tuts, wagging her finger at me.

'Dan was just ... He was just...' I muse out loud, dreamily recalling the marvellous poundings.

'Stop it! You're only tormenting yourself!' Brook interrupts.

She's right. I really must stop thinking about

those merry games of hide the sausage with Dan Elliott. Sniff, sniff.

Just as I psych myself up to actually do some work today, I catch sight of my reflection in the office window, hunched and inelegant, and do a double take.

'What?! I look like a bloody robin!' I huff. 'It's not fair! I was so looking forward to having a cute stuck-on bump like all the celebs, but I can already see I'm going to be one of the unlucky bastards who just gains weight everywhere and nobody can even tell they're pregnant!'

Brooke bursts out laughing, not even attempting to reassure me otherwise.

'How come it takes months on end to get a bit of weight off and a mere couple of weeks to look like Penguin in bloody Batman!' I wail, only making her laugh all the harder.

'Stop! Oh my God!' she pants breathlessly. 'One of these days I'm actually going to prolapse laughing at you!'

Delightful.

'That's it! No more sweets. No more baked goods. I'm done!' I declare, dropping myself heavily onto my office chair to make a start on the emails.

Two hours later I thrust a ten-dollar bill Brooke's way and ask her to pick up a bag of donuts and a chocolate brownie. Damn.

*****

Other women probably spend their days excitedly counting down to their wedding dress fittings, but I've been bloody dreading mine, and with good reason.

'Ugh! I can't, ugh, seem to ... get it past my chest!' I grunt, thrashing around in the bridal salon fitting room.

Reason 1.

'Don't force it or you'll tear it, you silly girl!' Duchess barks.

Reason 2.

'Goodness! You seem to have gone up at least a couple of dress sizes since we last saw you,' the bridal attendant remarks.

Bonus reason.

'Well, I *am* pregnant!' I rush to point out, my voice muffled from beneath the mass of gown stuck on my head.

'You're not carrying up below the bust though, darling. Besides, the baby's only the size of a prune,' Duchess sneers patronisingly.

Why is she here? She doesn't even like me! Why are we even doing this?

'I think it's probably best you take it off before it gets damaged, sweetie,' the bridal attendant soothes, patting my arm sympathetically.

'What now?' I pant, emerging like a sweaty, dishevelled phoenix from the ashes of my now cancelled couture gown.

'We'll have to find you something else. Of course, you do know you'll be paying for this gown too since it was made to order?' the attendant replies, wiping the smirk clean off Duchess's face.

'Yet more money wasted!' she groans.

'Oh yes, my fiancé says it's fine,' I reply, 'since he helped to get me in this condition in the first place.' I give Duchess a sideways glance.

'Let's look at some more traditional gowns, yes?' the attendant calls over her shoulder, already half out the room.

I soon observe that 'traditional' is a code word for stupendous, boring, tent-like gowns for the over fifty when minutes later bridal attendants are coming at me from all angles, shoving enormous meringue dresses under my nose.

'There we are, see? Much more suitable! This one is so Kate Middleton!' Duchess gushes, fondling the front of a silk, dark ivory embroidered gown.

Er, no! More like Sarah Ferguson.

'And what about this? It has sleeves. Perfect for hiding ham arms!'

Perfect for you, then! In fact, why don't you marry your son? I bet you would if you could!

'How about this one? A-line is the word for mums-to-be.'

Arseholes! There's a word for you!

'Well, I think you're being far too fussy.' Duchess finally scowls in defeat, folding her arms impatiently after I've seen all of four dresses.

'If you don't mind, I'd like to leave it for now and have a think,' I tell the attendant.

'Oh, er … No problem,' she mumbles, her face etched with disappointment at missing out on more of Brian's thousands.

'You can't be serious!' Duchess protests. 'We are mere months away from the big day. June will be here before we know it!'

'Thank you for your time.' I say with a smile, ignoring Duchess and breezing out of the store, hailing a cab and leaving her standing in the door of the bridal salon with her hands on her hips and an expression that screams 'Brian will get to hear about this in around three seconds time!'.

I spend the afternoon slumped on the sofa scrolling on my phone, anticipating Brian's arrival home from work. I can bet my arse Cruella already has him firmly on side.

A KIND OF TRAGIC WEDDING

Ooh, what's this? A Facebook friend request ... Ugh, that's a face I know well, grinning in an enormous green hat with Dad stood half concealed by it, only his feeble smile visible. What the fuck are *they* doing on here?! Tremendously late to the party, but still, I never thought I'd ever see Mother's mug on social media. I accept the request and proceed to stalk my own parents' page. Yes, this is how tragic it's got. I used to stalk the page of a certain Adonis, now I stalk the page of my own bloody parents! I don't know why I thought there might be anything interesting to look at, all I can see so far is a plethora of homemade cake photographs – exciting, if you're Mary Berry.

I observe the "active now" light and decide to give them a call on Messenger before I break the solemn vow I'd made never to look up Dan Elliott on here again.

It rings.

'Goodness, it can do calls as well?! Hello? Hello?'

It answers.

'Hi, Mother, it's me. I'm sat about at home and I noticed your friend request, so I thought I'd jus —'

'Yes, we're on Bookface now. Wonderful, isn't it?' she trills back before I can even finish my sentence.

'I didn't think social media was your thing,' I remind her.

'Well, quite a few of the ladies at the country club have Bookface so I thought, well, why not?'

'It's Facebook, Mother.'

'And do you know, I've gotten over twenty likes on my lemon drizzle cake. Fabulous, isn't it?'

'Yeah, great, Mother.'

'Well, yes, I rather think it is! Especially since Delia Davenport only got twelve likes on her red velvet.'

Oh, for fuck's sake, I might've guessed that woman would be involved in some way.

'Anyhow, now that we're Bookface friends, perhaps you wouldn't mind popping over to our page as soon as we're done here and liking my lemon drizzle? That would then take me to twenty-three likes, very nearly double Delia Davenport's scabby twelve!'

'Oh, for God's sa—'

'Now, don't swear dear, not when you're sat on such a grand sofa. Anyway, what's been happening with you? How are things?' Mother interrupts, taking me by complete surprise by actually asking about *me* for once.

I take a deep breath. There's a lot to say but

possibly only 0.5 of a second in which to say it. 'Well, Duchess invited herself along to my wedding dress fitting today and I couldn't get the dress on and she tried to take over and choose—'

'Do you know, if there's one thing I cannot stand it's overbearing people,' Mother interrupts. 'There's nothing worse than a control freak, there really isn't.'

I pause, almost choking on my own saliva.

'And we all knew the dress wasn't going to fit, dear, that's no surprise. You were piling it on the second after conception,' she adds mercilessly.

'Don't hold back, Mother, will you?' I mutter.

'Anyway, you were saying about that dreadful Duchess woman,' she prompts.

I try again. 'Yeah, well, to cut a long story short, she basically tried to choose the dress and when I wasn't having any of it, she turned nasty – well, even nastier than usual – to the point I had to walk out the store and a get a cab back to—'

'Do you know, I've never liked that woman from the moment I clapped eyes on her!' Mother interrupts. *Again.*

'Well, yes, I had gathered that, Moth—'

'It's all in the eyes dear, all in the eyes. Mirror to the soul they are. Oh yes, I've gotten very good at sussing out difficult people over the years,' she chuckles proudly.

Hm.

'Well, what are you going to do about it, dear?'

'I don't know, slip some cyanide into her tea?' I half joke.

'Not *her*, the dress, dear, the dress! You're the bride, you can't very well turn up in your birthday suit,' she trills.

'Well, I thought I'd—'

'Oh! I have the perfect solution!' she roars, making me jump in fright. 'Why don't I loan you my wedding dress, dear? It's an empire silhouette, a timeless lace classic! You'd only need a good seamstress to let it out a little and it would be simply—'

'NO!' I roar in horror, the very idea of wearing Mother's hideous eighties wedding dress a scarier prospect than walking down the aisle with my bare arse on display.

'Now, there's no need to shout dear, I'm not deaf.'

Nor am I, but I'm often left on the brink of it after Mother's phone calls.

'Well then, since you're so dead-set against taking practical advice, why don't you just take yourself off with Brian's credit card and make a jolly good day of it, dear. Take Brooke along. Do lunch!' she suggests.

'Well, I—'

She roars suddenly, shattering my poor nerves for the second time. 'Your father's out pressure-washing the drive and his trousers are ... Oh, for heaven's sake, his trousers are hanging halfway down his ... Oh no! Number twenty-two have just pulled into their driveway. I must go dear, before they see hi—'

Silence.

'Arse?' I muse out loud.

I glance at my screen.

"How was the quality of your call?" Messenger prompts.

Frowning, I give it one star – well, I didn't get a bloody word in edgeways, did I? Not the app's fault, but still.

Moments later, a message pops onto my screen:

Petunia Bradshaw: *Don't forget to like my lemon drizzle!*

The second Brian walks in through the front door after work, I can tell he's in Duch-ass mode. Call it a sixth bloody sense, although the sideways glance he gives along with his sullen trout expression is a dead giveaway. Pfft! I bet she had him ready on speed dial the second my cab pulled away earlier.

'Before you say anything, just know that it was all *her* doing!' I announce, folding my arms defensively.

'I really don't need this!' he mumbles as he walks away from me, not even waiting a moment to hear me out.

Yep! He's definitely on Team Cruella.

'You ignorant tosspot!' I yell after him, feeling a sudden sense of déjà vu as I tear off my engagement ring and throw it at him.

He stops dead, observing it sailing into and bouncing off the wall in front of him.

'There won't be another if you lose this one,' he warns, turning and looking down his nose at me as though I were a naughty child.

'Yeah? Well, who are you marrying Brian, me or your mother? 'Cos if you keep taking her side and allowing her to disrespect me, then I'm not bloody sure I want your ring on my finger, anyway!' I shout after him as he skulks off in the direction of the kitchen.

I stand scowling in his wake, instantly spying the butler's lurking shadow behind me through the reflection of the marble flooring. It quickly disappears. I'll bet this is the most action he's ever witnessed since he began working for Brian. God, he's probably already busy penning his memoirs: *What the Butler Saw*, or similar. Well, if things carry on like this, he'll soon have enough material for a sodding trilogy!

Chapter 5:

Sexual Healing

'Why is Tinder so wack?!' Brooke whinges, scrolling defeatedly through her phone at her desk. 'I must've had over ten thousand likes and not one of them is hot!'

'Ten thousand likes? You're too bloody fussy, mate,' I mumble, reaching my hand into the drawer of my desk for another gummy bear.

'Er, no I'm not! You wanna see some of the dorks on here,' she protests, holding out her phone to me.

I flick through, giving my verdict on each. 'Hm, *he's* a brute, *he* looks like a weirdo, *he's* a vain bastard, *he's* a scruffy sod ... Ooh, he's not bad,' I announce, holding out the phone.

'Not my type,' Brooke says dismissively, turning her nose up.

'So, what *is* your type, exactly?' I sigh. 'And do not say Tom Hardy, I'm sick of hearing about the bloke.'

She grabs her phone from me and loads up Facebook. 'Well, yes, in an ideal world it's Tom Hardy every time. But realistically speaking' – she taps away and then points her phone to me – 'him. He's very much my type,' she declares, pointing lustfully and going all doe-eyed at the profile pic of some hulk of a guy with a dashing grin, kitted out in American football gear.

'Well, get on it then!' I enthuse. 'Message him. Ask him out!'

'Well, I would, only he's dead,' she says, blunt as you like.

'He's dead?!' I gasp back at her, my mouth slowly falling open. 'Then you've more bloody chance with Tom Hardy!'

'Yeah, he died, like, two or three years ago of some terminal illness,' she reveals, stroking the screen thoughtfully. 'Such a waste ... such a terrible waste.'

'Ah, an old squeeze was he?' I ask sympathetically.

'Oh, no. I never knew him.'

'Right ... so he's basically a dead stranger, then?' I suggest, eyes widening in horror at what I'm hearing. My hand reaches into the drawer and I pop a few more gummy bears into my mouth as I wait for her to explain.

'Well, I'd seen his photo in some piece about him in the local newspaper and I thought wow, he's fit as fuck! So, I looked him up on Facebook, had a nose through his public pics and sort of got a bit attached from there. Every now and then I venture back to his page for an ogle.'

As you do.

'I just think we really could have been something, you know?' she goes on. 'I mean, if I'd have known him and he wasn't dead.'

I pause, trying not to choke on several gummy bears.

'How about we go through your Tinder likes again?' I swiftly suggest, snatching the phone.

'But they're a load of shmucks!' she whines.

'Well as long as they've a pulse, I reckon it's a start!'

By close of play, we still haven't found Brooke a potential match.

'What about this one? He seems kinda cool,' she remarks, holding up his photo.

'Is he wearing make-up?' I frown. 'I have to know that shade of lipstick! Why don't you message him to ask?'

'Piss off!'

'Oh, go on. It'd be a good ice-breaker!'

*****

During the drive home, I enter a deep state of contemplation. Here's Brooke spending her days ogling the dead while I'm engaged to be married to a handsome billionaire – an insufferable mummy's boy, *perhaps* – but a handsome billionaire all the same, who is very much alive and kicking … except in the bedroom department. I really must give thought to how fortunate I am more often … except for in the bedroom department.

Crap sex in mind and even though I am indeed pregnant, I conclude we're far too early into our relationship to let things slip by the wayside. I set about coming up with ways to spice things up beyond closing my eyes and pretending he's Dan Elliott. Well, we always seem to do it in bed with the lights off on a Sunday night. Maybe if we were to do it on a different day, in a different setting, at a different time, it might just do the trick!

Arriving home before Brian, my first objective is to send that nosy bastard butler packing.

'I'll be cooking tonight so you can get off early,' I tell him pleasantly.

'Mr Garcia hasn't said anything to that effect,' he counters, as though the word of Mrs Garcia – or as good as – isn't enough.

Yes, well I'm telling you now,' I reply, pleasantness depleting rapidly.

'If I could just clear it with the Mr Garcia first …'

Mate, it may not look like it when I'm throwing engagement rings and crying in the orangery, but you should know that *I* am the only boss round here!

'No, actually, you can't. I'm organising a surprise for him,' I quickly tell him.

'Oh, what's the surprise?' he fishes.

Oh, just me with no clothes on … nothing you haven't seen before. Nosey shit!

God, people are so brazen these days. I would never dream of prying into others' affairs like this clown is mine!

'It's just a surprise dinner.' I frown, glancing at my phone after it tinkles with an alert from the tracking app Brian and I each have installed on our phones.

Brian has left Wilson Garcia & Co, Manhattan.

Right, you need to piss off now!

'Oh, then why don't I stay to help you with that?' he suggests.

Er, no mate. This is one thing that will *not* find its way into *What the Butler Saw*!

Christ, he doesn't give up easily, does he? I

was of the thinking that butlers are trained to hover invisibly in the background, appearing like magic when needed and fucking off quickly when required. Looks like ours needs some training.

Bugger off, you, persistent sod; I'm trying to save my flagging sex life, here!

'No, honestly, but, thank you,' I insist, willing him with every fibre of my being to get gone.

Eventually, he does.

With the butler having done one, I quickly take myself off upstairs to get my kit off and freshen up. Glancing at my watch, I calculate I have just enough time to pull this off before Brian arrives home.

I touch up my make-up, mist the air with *Coco Mademoiselle* before walking through it, throw on a towelling bathrobe over my birthday suit and peg it downstairs to the kitchen looking for matches. Having located these with little fuss, I tear through to the front room where I'm pleased to see the butler has left a nicely stoked fire in the hearth. I set about lighting the candles and finding some music to set the ambience. Flicking through Brian's music collection, I quickly find myself stumped. Well, other than for "Jump" by Van Halen or whatever the name is, I can't find anything that sounds naughty. Ah, hang on, here's some Marvin Gaye. I don't know his music but apparently people associate it with shagging.

Right, now, where should I be? What should I be doing? Should I stand? Sit? Hmm, sitting would be the safer choice since my birthday suit isn't what it was. What if I sit naked on the coffee table in front of the fire? It'll be all romantic in the soft, flattering glow of the candlelight and proper kinky, since he won't be expecting it. He'll probably arrive home expecting another blazing row about his mother, then he'll walk in to find the only thing we'll be having is blazing hot sex! Ha!

Observing car lights coming down the driveway, I make doubly sure it's his car – which it definitely is – before rushing to get into position. Whipping off my bathrobe, I chuck it across the room, smashing a vase off the sideboard in the process, then proceed to perch seductively on the coffee table, facing the fire with my back to the doorway.

My perfect posture slumps somewhat as I continue to wait … and wait. Ugh, where the hell is he?! Eventually, hearing his key in the front door, I quickly flip my hair, cross my legs, and arch my back to look sexy. The front door closes behind him and I hear the click-clack of his footsteps approaching upon the marble flooring. They stop abruptly on reaching the sitting room.

'Don't say a word, just screw me to the wall!'

I order in a put-on sexy voice, keeping my back turned.

Silence.

'Or haven't you got the stamina?' I mock, in a deep and sultry tone after a bit of a pause.

'Well, twenty years ago, I might've had,' comes a very un-Brian-like voice.

Spinning around in horror, my heart stops as I observe Howard Wilson, Brian's elderly business partner, stood in the sitting room doorway looking pale and clammy as though he might keel over and go into cardiac arrest at any moment. Oh, bugger me blind! No! Fuck no!

A bastard of a silence ensues, other than for Marvin's warbling. Well, I think I've just established that, if anything, sexual healing is something that's too much fucking hassle! I don't think I'll bloody bother in future.

'Brian gave me his keys,' the poor chap quickly explains, not knowing where to look. 'H-he said ... He said to just go on in and make myself at home.'

Did he now?! Hmph! Typical Brian with his *mi casa es tu casa*.

'He's, er, out in the car taking a business call,' Harold continues, grabbing onto the door for support while I race to cover my modesty and turn Marvin off.

'I'm terribly sorry,' I pant, mortified, 'Brian didn't tell me he was bringing anyone back here.'

He waves his hand dismissively as though to suggest I should think nothing of it. Hmm, that's rather a big ask. The only thing I shall think nothing of will be stringing Brian up later!

'Do excuse me!' I gulp, grabbing the bathrobe, flinging it on and hurtling out of the room.

*****

'How in the hell was I to know you were planning to greet me in the nude?' Brian argues during his dressing-down after Howard's departure.

'Well, well I wish you would stop bringing people back to the bloody house unannounced!' I protest.

'Honey, I have to. It's business. You wouldn't understand.'

'I understand business perfectly well, I'm a fucking entrepreneur!' I roar, my face twitching at the nerve of him.

'I didn't mean it like that. I meant that it's customary in business to bring people over to the house on occasion. We had some stuff to go through and we ran over. I didn't want to be late home, so I brought Howard back here to finish up,' he explains, fatigued.

'Well, you might've called or dropped me a text as a minimum!' I argue.

'I'm CEO, for Christ's sake! I can't be seen to be calling home all the time. It just implies I'm pussy-whipped and that's not good for business. People would start trying to walk all over me,' he reasons.

'What, you mean like mummy does?!' I scoff, raising my brows mockingly.

'Ah. How didn't I guess this is all down to your problem with Mom,' he sighs, taking off his tie and throwing it across the room.

'Er, *my* problem with *her*? I'd say it's the other bloody way round!' I scream at him as he storms out the bedroom, slamming the door in my face.

Wow, all I'd wanted was for us to have some lovely sex together and this is what happens. I feel like we're heading for a decree absolute … and we're not even fucking married, yet!

I spend much of the rest of the evening sulking in an enormous bubble bath, thinking that something's got to give. Why can't Brian see that his mother has unfairly taken issue with me since day one? She doesn't even try to be nice. She's horrible to me in front of him, which speaks volumes about how she treats me behind his back. Why can't he see it? *Why*?!

In terms of our non-marital marital issues, I reckon I could slap down the workaholic in Brian a bit and the crap sex can be worked on, but I don't know where to bloody start where Duchess is concerned. Evil is as evil does, after all. I don't know, perhaps I could take her out to lunch someplace nice and win her over somehow. Assure her that I'm not about to steal her precious son away from her and appeal to her better nature – not that I'm at all sure she even has one. Ah, well. Sometimes in life you have to speculate to accumulate. If some flowers and lunch on me wins me an agreeable future mother-in-law, then it's well worth a shot.

Climbing out of the bath, I notice I've cut my leg. I really must stop re-using crap, disposable razors. I pause, frowning in contemplation. No, hang on a minute. I didn't even bother shaving tonight on account of the silent vow I'd made to withhold all sex from Brian going forward as his punishment. As far as I'm concerned, a woman who's not having sex is a woman who needn't shave. So, what's this blood, then?

Hurriedly, I grab some toilet roll and wipe between my legs, not thinking for a minute it's coming from there. My heart freezes in my chest as I discover it is. Oh, God. No. Please, no!

The room spins as I wrap myself in a towel and walk slowly downstairs in a dripping-wet daze toward the front room where Brian is sitting tapping away on his laptop. He doesn't even look up as I appear in the doorway, probably assuming it's a crap second attempt at seduction.

'Brian, I...' I trail off, not sure how to find the words to tell him I may be losing our baby as we speak.

His expression changes on observing the fear etched on my face. 'What is it?' he asks nervously.

'I'm b-bleeding,' I whisper, sinking to my knees at the mere sound of those words.

*****

'Elizabeth Bradshaw?' comes a voice from somewhere in the distance.

In normal circumstances, I cringe whenever my name is called out in public. Other people's names sound perfectly normal to me, but I've always felt mine sounds silly and chumpish for some reason. As a kid, my name was such a big thing to me. I'd put so much focus on it, like that time I changed my name to Kate Anderton for a week but no sod complied. Now as I sit in the hospital waiting room with Brian beside me, a chumpish name is the very least of my worries.

'Lizzie, that's us, come on,' Brian prompts, taking my hand as we rise in tandem from our seats.

'Hey there, follow me.' The waiting nurse smiles meekly.

The silence is deafening as she leads us into a small side room. The silence continues until she attempts to draw some blood from my arm for testing, at which point I suddenly get a bit vocal.

'Um, could I lie down please, I'm, er, not so good with needles,' I whimper.

'Yah, sure,' the nurse replies, peering down at the pawprint tattoo on my wrist I'd had done in Smudge's memory and raising a brow.

Oh, that? That was for decorative purposes. This is you stealing the blood from within my veins. This is scary!

'Okay, tiny scratch,' she warns, prompting my entire body to jerk, knocking the needle clean out of her hand and onto the floor.

'Lizzie, come on now. We need to get this done,' Brian sighs, making me feel like an eight-year-old while the nurse rattles about in the trolley beside her for another needle.

Eventually, with me facing the wall and warning her repeatedly that I do not wish to see the filled vial afterwards, she fills it.

'There we are, see? Nothing to it,' she dismisses in a cooey voice, taping a cotton wool ball to my scary pinprick wound.

Er, no love. There's *everything* to it when you've a phobia of blood and veins!

I turn back around from the wall, instantly spotting the vial of my blood resting in the polystyrene tray on her lap which she hasn't bothered her arse to conceal from me as requested. Ugh! It all but waves at me, yelling 'Look, Lizzie! This is your blood speaking. Look at me, all dark crimson and yucky! I came from your veins, I did.'

'What now?' Brian asks.

'Well, I'll get this off for testing and we'll look at the hormone levels in the sample. That'll give us an idea of what's what, and I'm going to try to get you in for a scan,' she replies. 'Although, with it being late in the day we might be looking at tomorrow now,' she adds, glancing at her pocket watch. 'Try not to worry, a lot of women go on to have healthy pregnancies after some bleeding,' she says, observing my angst-ridden face on her way out.

While I am obviously very worried about what's going on, my doom-face is actually in part due to the fact I feel faint from that sodding ordeal I just went through. I'm not fussed about the "I've been brave" sticker, but I wouldn't say no to a lollipop if there's one going.

We sit in numb silence for a bit.

'I'm gonna grab a coffee. Would you, er, like anything?' Brian asks, rising from his chair.

For most Brits, a good old cup of tea is often the first thing to do in a crisis, as though it's some amazing go-to fix for everything. I turn to vodka, personally. Oh, but not today.

'No, thank you,' I whisper, shaking my head.

'Okay, be right back,' he mumbles, disappearing out through the door.

I sit staring at the grey linoleum floor, listening to the blend of hushed voices among the comings and goings of busy footsteps outside the room. It's all in a day's work for medical professionals, but just being here can bring about the end of the world for some people.

All hospitals have that same smell, don't they? Clinical. All rubber gloves and disinfectant. It's not an unpleasant smell, but nor is it a good smell, since you only smell it while in hospital and if you're in hospital, it's seldom for anything good. Fortunately for me, it's not a place I've had to often go, but it's somewhere I need to be right now as I sit desperate for answers.

'Please be okay, little bean,' I whisper, rubbing my belly and feeling completely powerless, knowing that whatever will be will be and there's not a thing Brian, I, nor anyone else can do about it. All we can do is wait and hope.

I look up at the door as it squeaks open minutes later. It's just Brian, back from the hot drinks machine.

'Any news yet?' he asks.

I shake my head.

'Mom sends her best,' he tells me apprehensively.

Oh, dear. Duchess knows already. Is there *anything* he doesn't report back to her? It's a wonder he doesn't call her after he ejaculates, just so she's included!

I nod but say nothing. Now isn't the time. The nurse walks in moments later, further re-enforcing that notion.

'Okay, if you'd like to follow me, they're going to get you scanned over in the ultrasound department,' she says, holding open the door.

Having spent all this time waiting for her return, I'm now unsure I want to even go.

'Right. I'm going to need a brief period of quiet while I gather all the information I need from the scan. After this, I'll talk you through my findings and answer any questions you may have, okay?' the sonographer advises, proceeding to move the probe across my tummy.

I take a deep breath, my heart pounding as Brian reaches across the bed for my hand.

'I can't look,' I mouth at him, keeping my head turned away from the screen.

Less than a minute on, I have the answer without even needing to look. It's written all over Brian's face.

'I'm sorry to tell you, there's no heartbeat,' the sonographer finally confirms.

My world crashes down in bits around me. I stare up at the ceiling as those words hit, snatching the last ounce of wind from my sails. Tears prick as I battle a mix of gut-wrenching emotions from disbelief, to guilt, to denial, to grief, to contempt, rage, and back round again in one big loop. Was it something I did? Could I have done something or not done something to have prevented it? Was it stress? The arguing with Brian? I don't understand it. Why? Just why?!

'I'm very sorry for your loss,' the sonographer says gently, wiping down my belly with a paper towel. 'Is there anything you'd like to ask? Do you have any questions?'

Oh, more than she'd be able to answer in her lifetime.

When I can finally bring myself to move, I look over toward Brian. It's the first time I've seen him cry.

'I j-just want to know w-why,' I answer eventually.

'Ah, I'm afraid I don't know the answer to that. Nobody ever does.' She sighs. 'Miscarriage is incredibly common. We see it so many times here and I don't think I've met a woman yet who hasn't wanted an answer to that question. I only wish we knew.'

'B-but we saw the heartbeat just last week,' I point out. 'What could go wrong in a week?'

She presses her lips together and shrugs. 'Just know that it's unlikely to be anything you did or didn't do. Most commonly, it's down to a genetic abnormality,' she explains, launching into a long spiel laced with medical terminology in an attempt at reassuring us.

It doesn't.

I'd never given miscarriage much thought before. I was pretty ignorant to it until, like a bolt out of the blue, I just became one of the many people to fall victim to it. I guess it stands to reason since you can never fully understand anything until you experience it for yourself. But I know now that when I hear it spoken about in future, it will be a word that stirs a knowing grief within me – a grief which, sadly, so many others know well.

Chapter 6:

Best Laid Plans

The ping of a text alert wakes me from what must've been the worst night's sleep of my life. I glance at the time on my phone: 11.11am. Then the text:

Lillibeth, Brian's just told us the news. We're heartbroken for you both. Always here for shed-based fatherly life counselling if you want to talk about it. Take care of yourself. Love you. Dad x

They know.

I roll over and stare at the ceiling. Suddenly, I don't know what to do with myself or how to even start the day. My objectives were so clear before: work, midwife appointments, wedding appointments, eating for four. The future had been so certain. Now, it seems so bleak. It's as though it's pointless even getting out of bed. I just feel so empty inside.

'Morning,' Brian greets me with a small smile, hovering in the bedroom door. 'Thought I'd come up and check to see if you're awake yet.'

I return his smile, stumped for words.

'I know it's a shitty question, but how're you feeling?' he asks, walking slowly over toward the bedside.

Do I even need to answer that?

'Like the world's ended,' I mumble glumly.

'Same,' he agrees, sitting down on the edge of the bed. 'It was the first thing to hit me when I woke this morning that I'm ... that I'm no longer a father-to-be,' he says, his voice breaking as he turns his head away from me.

All at once, it dawns on me that I'm not alone in my bubble of grief. Brian is very much beside me. *Yes*, I was carrying our baby. *Yes*, I'm the one having the miscarriage. But the loss is shared, along with the barrage of emotions that come with it.

I sit up and place a hand on his shoulder. I haven't any words of comfort. None exist. I've known grief before, but this is a very different kind. When loved ones die, the funeral is the last goodbye. A designated occasion at which to pay our respects. To remember them. To share memories. To give thanks for their lives. It's also the point from which we try to move forward with our own. Beyond this, we have our memories to remember them by. With a miscarriage, there is no body to lay to rest. No funeral. We didn't know the life lost. Never got to meet them and never will. How can we remember them when there aren't any memories? All we have is a single scan picture. We didn't even get to know what we were having. It seems so abrupt. So cold. So final.

'You know, ever since Dad walked out on us when I was a kid, I knew that when I became a father myself I would be to my child everything that was missing from my own childhood,' Brian tells me out of nowhere, shielding his eyes with his hand, his head hung.

I had known his father left when he was very young, but he'd never let on how it had affected him, until now.

'I was so ready to be everything my own father wasn't.' He sighs, quickly wiping away the tears that are forming in droves – whether he likes it or not – before they've a chance to fall.

'And you will be someday,' I tell him, welling up myself. 'Just not this time around.'

*****

Two days on from the miscarriage, Brian goes back to work. I don't resent him for it. I know that throwing himself into work is a welcome distraction for him; it's just his way of dealing with things. I, on the other hand, am not ready to plan the weddings of excited, blissfully happy couples just yet. In stark contrast to work being a distraction for Brian, my line of work only serves as a reminder of how unhappy I am, and not just at losing the baby. The shed-based fatherly counselling session I find myself engaged in with Dad that afternoon only further highlights it.

'I'm so sorry, love,' he says for the umpteenth time. 'I know you weren't over the moon with the baby news when you first found out, but I could see how happy you were after the scan.'

I nod in agreement.

'How're you bearing up?'

'Well, I'm not, to be honest,' I tell him, welling up. 'Brian's gone back to work. I'm here in the house on my tod. It just feels so personal, you know? Like, there's no body to be buried so it's almost like we're mourning nothing, even though it was everything. I feel like there's nothing to show for the pain I'm feeling.'

'I can imagine, love,' he sighs. 'And there's nothing I nor anyone else can say or do to make it any better. The only thing that can help you is time. Time is a great healer.'

'I know, Dad. But, well …'

'It's not just the baby, is it?' he suggests, his fatherly sixth sense guessing correctly.

I bite my lip. 'It made everything easier, Dad. It kept the façade going. The baby was the only thing keeping me attached to Brian.' I sigh, feeling terrible. 'I feel like now there's no baby, I'm getting more and more distant from him by the day.'

He nods, empathetically. 'Well, that's understandable.'

'God, I feel so bad, Dad. I feel awful for feeling like this.'

'You will do, love. But it's like I told you before, there's only so long you can live a lie. It might seem the done thing to do putting other people first to keep them happy, but in the end everyone's unhappy anyway and all you've done is prolong the agony,' he says, clicking his tongue thoughtfully.

'You're right, I know you're right, but he's grieving, Dad. The wedding's getting closer and closer. We've got all this stuff arriving by the truckload. I don't know what to do!' I groan, my heart sinking.

'I know, love. I've got your mother running around like a headless bloody chicken organising this, that and the other,' he says, and I can almost hear him looking around, making sure she's not within earshot. 'Ah, dear, you're between a rock and a hard place, aren't you? But, well ...'

'What?'

'Well, you must know you can't marry him, surely?'

In theory, yes, but having watched Brian's heart break over the past few days, I'd have to be some bitch to break it all over again. This wedding *has to* go ahead. I've no choice.

*****

Rattling about isolated in a house that has never really felt like home provokes a whole lot of soul searching. Do I love Brian? Yes. Am I in love with Brian? No. Is it possible to make yourself fall in love with someone? Not sure. Is generic love going to be enough? Don't know.

It seems ironic. I have all the makings for a happy life in front of me, but I'm not happy. It's like having all the ingredients for a magnificent cake, but no matter how closely you follow the instructions, it just won't turn out like the picture on the recipe card. Something's not working. Something's not right.

Just when I think my anguish has reached max scale, Duchess shows up at the door armed with a small floral basket of simple white flowers and no more a glum expression than usual. Ugh, if there was one person in the world I really didn't wish to be in the company of anytime soon, she's it! No offence.

With little choice, I invite her in.

'Hello, Lizzie. I told Brian I'd come by and see how you're doing,' she says, stepping forward, grabbing me by the shoulders, and giving me a wooden three-second hug on her way inside.

'Hi, Veronica. Thank you. It's good of you to come,' I greet her, taking the basket.

Well, I suppose it was nice of her to check in on me and bring me flowers, but I know from experience that it's only a matter of seconds until she pisses me off.

'So, how are you?' she asks.

BOOM! She's managed it already.

'Um, not too good, Veronica,' I mumble with a discreet eye roll, leading the way into the front room.

'Well, it's like I was saying to Brian on the phone, it could've been worse, darling. Could've been *much* worse,' she says, aggressively plumping the cushions before she's even prepared to sit her haughty arse on the sofa. 'I know women who've lost babies far further into their pregnancies than you were yours. Very unpleasant business. They have to have these operations, you know, to clear everything away. You're actually very fortunate to be able to pass yours naturally at home,' she says, leaving me totally speechless. 'My sister had to give birth to a stillborn,' she adds casually, craning her neck to look for the butler.

I stare at her, dumbfoundedly.

'What? Did I say something wrong?' she asks, returning her attention to me, completely oblivious to the cruel insensitivity of her words.

In the grand scheme of things, she may be right. There'll always be someone who's had it worse, but when is it ever helpful or appropriate to devalue a person's pain? Is there no end to this woman's shortcomings? There's certainly no beginning to her virtues, that's for bloody sure!

'Well, there are some things you just don't say to a woman who's sat opposite you having a miscarriage as you speak,' I tell her as calmly as possible, mustering every ounce of strength not to smother her with the cushions she just spent a lifetime re-arranging.

'Well, I'm sorry if you feel like that,' she mumbles dismissively, as though my being an overly-sensitive being is the problem, rather than her lack of empathy, awful way with words, and distinct lack of tact.

Quite how I go on to get through coffee with the cow is beyond me. It's amazing the challenges us humans can overcome when pushed to the very brink.

My next monumental challenge comes in forcing a smile when Brian announces over dinner that he doesn't want to 'hang around' and we should 'start trying again for another baby as soon as we can'.

*****

When, some weeks later, I've finally managed to re-master the life skills required to get up, get clean, and get from A to B without having a breakdown, I decide to go into work. With it being a Friday, it would have made more sense to go back at the start of the working week, but I've got to get out of this place before I go stir-crazy.

Brooke doesn't let me get an inch through the door before lunging at me and flinging her arms around my neck, holding me in a vice-like hug that goes on and on. She doesn't let go, not even when I attempt to walk to my desk with all her bodyweight literally hanging off my neck as I drag her along with me.

'It's so good to have you back,' she says, pulling away finally. 'Obviously because of what's happened and all, but I do need to just fess up that I've had a little incident with the fax machine,' she adds, looking nervous.

'What?'

'Well, you know that guy on Tinder? I went on, like, one date with him, right? And he was weird as hell! Like, I swear he was wearing *Daisy* by Marc Jacobs! I like, *totally* know that smell! I wore it all through eleventh grade, right? I know Daisy when I smell it. So, anyway, I thought I'd give him a chance, you know 'cos anything goes these days, so, like, maybe it's prudish to just expect guys to stick to Hugo Boss?

'Anyway, it's not like I got any better offers and beggars can't be choosers, right? So, yeah, he texted me at work yesterday with this weird request for me to sit on the photocopier and fax the result to him and I sort of agreed to it just to shut him up, you know? 'Cos like, my phone was pinging every second and I've got this total bridezilla making all these demands and stuff. You know what the silly bitch wanted? She only wanted me to hire Tom Hardy to walk her down the fucking aisle! I'm like, bitch, please! You think I can just call up Tom Hardy? You don't even wanna know what I'd say to Tom Hardy if I could get him on the phone. I'd be fucking arrested! And if Tom Hardy was walking *me* down the aisle, *my* wedding wouldn't even go ahead, 'cos I'd be mounting him right there on the aisle carpet in front of my groom! Well, he's just so hot, isn't he, Tom Hardy? I mean, like, who doesn't want intercourse with Tom Hardy?! Ugh, I totally need a man like Tom Hard—'

'You've knackered the fax machine, haven't you?' I interject with a sigh.

'Yeah,' she replies ashamedly, her face dropping. 'I thought it would easily hold my weight, right? But it, well, it didn't. So, like, we can't do any printing or photocopying or faxing now until we get another. But he's blocked! I mean, *Daisy*-man, I've blocked him. So, um, it won't happen again.'

I stare at her for a few moments, my eyes welling.

'Hey, it's okay, we can find another one just as dope!' she soothes, flinging an arm around my shoulders.

'I couldn't give a bloody toss about the fax machine,' I half sob, half laugh.

'You're not mad?' she gasps, breathing a sigh of relief.

Mad? No. But *she* is, and mad is good. Boy, have I missed that!

Rather than doing any actual work to arrange other people's unions, we find ourselves embroiled in conversation vis-à-vis my own which is looming on the horizon.

'So, you don't want to try again for more kids with Brian?' Brooke asks, kicked back in her office chair with her legs resting up on the desk in front of her.

'No, I'm going to go straight back on the pill,' I reply, looking down, guiltily.

'Why?' she asks.

I sit picking my nails in glum silence.

'You don't love him, do you?' she suggests.

I hesitate before shaking my head woefully. 'Not as I should.'

'Oof!' she remarks, taking a deep inhalation of breath. 'But what about the wedding? We're into spring now. June's coming around real fast.'

I sigh, head in hands. 'I know that! Christ, I can't think about anything else.'

'Girl, you gotta tell him how you feel,' she says, as though it would be the simplest thing in the world.

'How can I? He's grieving for our lost baby. I can't go and dump this on him too, that would be so cruel!'

'It's gonna be way crueller later down the line when you walk five minutes into the marriage – you're gonna, you *know* you're gonna! And when you do, you'll be taking half of everything he's got with you. People are gonna think you married him just to get at his fortune,' she says, making a very valid point and one I hadn't considered up until now.

'But I would never do that! Just snatch and grab everything he's worked for half his life for? That's so not me!'

'I know it's not, but that's how it'll look.'

'Oh, fuck! I couldn't bear for Brian to think of me like that,' I say, sinking back into my chair despondently.

'Hmm, and that Duchess is gonna want your head on a fucking stick!' Brooke tuts.

'I think she already wants that now,' I reply numbly, staring into space.

'Well, the longer you leave it, the harder it's gonna be,' she announces, stating the bleeding obvious.

With Brooke having given me some food for thought – adding to the sodding banquet I already have – I spend the drive home from work rehearsing imaginary crisis talks with Brian:

Me: Can we talk, Brian?

Brian: Sure, what is it, honey?

Me: I'm not in love with you and I can't marry you.

Director: CUT! Too cold. Way too cold!

Take two. And, action!

Me: Brian, there's no easy way to say this, but I can't marry you.

Brian: What? Why?

Me: Because I'm just not in love with you. Oh and I leave tonight.

Director: CUT! Still too damn cold! Can't you be a bit nicer about it? You know, softly softly?

Me: What would softly softly sound like?

Director: You gotta do it like this. 'Hey Brian, can we talk? Listen, Brian, there's no easy way to say this, but I'm having second thoughts about the wedding. You're a wonderful man and I care deeply about you, really I do, but I can't marry you because my heart's not in it and you deserve so much more than I can give you'.

Me: Wow! That's actually pretty good!

Director: Well, they don't pay me the big bucks for nothing!

Me: You *do* know this is just an imaginary conversation?!

Director: Oh yeah. Still good though, wasn't I?

Deep in thought with adrenalin surging through me, I ascend the long, lantern-lit sweeping driveway a little faster than I ought to – such that bits of gravel are flying about the place as I go – and proceed to park up, reversing aggressively into a bush and leaving a bit of a hole. Bugger. This top of the range Mercedes SL Roadster complete with techy parking aid is totally wasted on me.

Relieved that Brian's car is absent from the drive, I reach across to the passenger seat, grab my phone from my bag and sit, frantically texting Brooke.

Me: *I'm doing it tonight x*

Brooke: *OMG! But well done. Come crash here if you need some place to go after x*

Me: *I will, thanks. Wish me luck! x*

Brooke: *Good luck! x*

Flinging open the wardrobe doors, I rake through my massive accumulation of bags, looking for something big enough to shove a few of my things in to allow for a quick exit once the deed's done. Well, I don't fancy hanging around after dropping such a clanger! I'll organise for all my stuff sent on to Brooke's place later.

I spy the massive, fake Louis Vuitton tote of yesteryear and am suddenly overcome with an enormous sense of nostalgia, a showreel of embarrassing scenes from the past playing out in my mind.

'We've been through some scrapes together, haven't we?' I muse, fondling it vacantly. It seems only fitting that we should embark on my latest drama together, for old time's sake.

Wait, was I just talking to a handbag? Oof! I was!

Bag packed and shaking like a leaf, I take one last look around the bedroom.

'Goodbye massive, comfy bed,' I say with a sigh, brushing the posh, sateen covers. 'Bye dressing table,' I whisper, running my fingers along the polished wood. 'Goodbye fuck-off grand staircase,' I mumble, vacating the room and sliding my hand down the banister.

Aware that this is probably the last time I'll ever walk down such a magnificent set of stairs, I spontaneously take the opportunity to descend like a queen, lifting my posture and taking each step with the quintessence of grace, imagining a lobby full of courtiers bowing before me. It all starts off regal enough, but weighed down with the massive fake Louis tote and in true Lizzie Bradshaw style, I miscalculate my footing and slide down the last eight steps on my back, my head jerking violently as I bounce off each step with my expletives reverberating very un-queen-like across the entrance hall. Arrrgh, Christ, my coccyx!

As the headlights of Brian's car approach the house, I haul myself to my feet – pleased to note that I can't have broken my back – and dump the massive, fake Louis tote to the side of the front door. I take myself off into the sitting room where I perch anxiously on the edge of the sofa, heart pounding and back throbbing as I brace myself to break the heart of someone I genuinely care about.

I hear his key in the door and instantly recall Marvin-gate, hoping and praying Howard Wilson or similar isn't about to stroll into the house and fuck up my plans for the second time. I turn my head and give a sideways glance toward the door. He's alone, phew! But, ugh, I feel sorry for him already and that's just seeing his side profile. I haven't even said a bloody word yet! Oh God, why is life such a bitch?

'Hey, honey!' he chirps, walking into the front room. 'Am I pleased to see you! I have great news!' he announces.

I look up at him with pre-emptive half smile, though I know that whatever it is won't be great news to me. Well, not unless he's about to willingly invite me to walk out of his life with no hard feelings.

'I've been thinking about us and, well … I know my head's been in business too much lately. I haven't been there for you like I should have,' he begins, 'and, er … I know I haven't been very forthcoming, shall we say, in the bedroom department.'

I nod, wondering where all this is heading as my escape plan waits, tapping its foot impatiently at the forefront of my mind.

'Well, I'm gonna make it up to you. I've organised a trip to Paris this weekend! Private jet, The Ritz, the whole works! I thought we could use some alone time, just the two of us.' He smiles, crouching down to my level and sliding a hand up my leg suggestively. 'Plus, I got you an appointment with an excellent French bridal designer to help with the whole dress drama,' he adds, beginning to stroke my now very tense leg.

'I thought a little getaway might, you know, help things along with the baby-making.'

Before I can say a word, he launches himself at me and starts kissing me, passionately. I mean, really passionately. *Filthy* passionately. Whoa, hello! This is a different Brian. This is a *very* different Brian!

Then I'm following him back up the fuck-off grand staircase like a sheep and, less than thirty seconds later, find myself arse-naked upon the massive, comfy bed I had bid farewell to only a few minutes ago, not knowing whether I'm coming or going – literally.

Later...

Brooke: *Have you done it? x*

Me: *No in terms of leaving. Yes in terms of shagging x*

Brooke: *Oh, dear! x*

Chapter 7:

C'est la Vie

My phone buzzes with Mother's incoming call at the side of the bed, waking me from a filthy dream I was having about Dan Elliott. Shit, for three reasons:

1. The sordid Dan-dreams have started again.
2. I'm on what I've decided is a make-or-break romantic weekend getaway with Brian, during which I am lying beside him dreaming about being pummelled by another man. *Going well then!*
3. My bloody Mother wants to get at me at what is only ... ugh ... 7.02am.

'Yeah,' I answer, with a yawn, creeping out of bed into the en suite so as not to wake Brian.

'Oh, do stop answering the telephone like that, it's dreadfully common!' comes the shrill. 'Now, tell me how it went with Pierre Dupont, dear! I've been so excited! Everybody at the country club has been asking about the dress. They're positively itching to know who's designing it, dear, they really are! Well, of course, you know me, I haven't said a word about it, dear, just that there was a slight hitch with the first gown so you've flown out to Paris this weekend by private jet for an appointment with a famous bridal designer,' she says, all in one breath.

'Mother, it's 7.02am, I haven't even been to the bloody appointment yet!'

'Oh, I thought France is ahead of UK time, dear.'

'Yeah, by an hour, not half a sodding day!'

'Oh. Well, I'm glad I caught you before the appointment anyway, because I can give you a few pointers on etiquette and how to behave properly around important people, dear.'

'He's only a bridal designer, Mother,' I say with a sigh, 'not Nelson bleeding Mandela!'

'Of course, he's not. Mandela's dead, dear. Anyhow, I've just posted some photographs on Bookface from Daddy and I's weekend away in the Lake District and I haven't had a single like as yet! I've no idea why. I can't understand it. It's the weekend, where *is* everybody?!'

At what is now around 6.06am in the United Kingdom on a Saturday morning, in bloody bed I would imagine!

'Well, I suppose I could have had one or two

while I've been on the phone,' she continues. 'I'd better go and check and *you'd* better go and get yourself shipshape and Bristol for Pierre Dupont, dear. Call me the minute you've left your appointment, the very minute, you hear?'

'Yes, Mother, goodb—'

'Oh, and give our Lake District album a like as soon as you've hung up!'

Beep-beep-beep.

She's gone.

Ugh, I give up. I can't escape Mother in London, I can't escape her in New York and I sure as hell can't escape her in Paris!

When I'd agreed to come here to Paris with Brian – well, not *agreed* agreed, more like "allowed him to roger me when I was about to leave him last night, then just went with the flow" agreed – I didn't once give thought to the fact that I can't speak French. I'd had it in mind that this was to be a quickie weekend of eating, shopping, and shagging that I wouldn't need to be fluent in the lingo for. How bloody wrong was I?

The infamous Pierre bloody Dupont, as it happens, speaks pretty much sod-all English, which I find out less than fifteen seconds into my appointment at his boutique. Now, as he ponces about gabbling a load of French at me, all I can do is smile and nod. He suddenly goes quiet and stares at me intently.

Eh? Oh! I think he's waiting for an answer to whatever the hell it was he just said.

'Er, *je non parlour de France*,' I tell him, some vague recollection I have of Dad saying it umpteen times on a trip to the Alps when I was a teenager.

'*Quelle?*'

Shit.

'*Je* dress, *por favour*,' I try, hoping that's enough to get him to bring out some sample gowns.

He shoots me a strange look and begins taking my measurements in silence while I stand with furrowed brows, wondering how on earth this appointment can possibly proceed.

I leave the boutique an hour later with an invoice for fuck knows what in my hand.

'Hey! How'd it go, honey? You get a dress?' Brian chirps as I wander into the bar back at The Ritz where he's sat with a drink, tapping away on his laptop.

'Er … I'm not sure,' I mumble, still befuddled by the whole experience. But one thing's for sure, I'm not about to go and add to it by calling Mother as she'd demanded.

'How can you not be sure if you bought a

dress?' Brian asks, pulling a face.

'Well, he didn't speak any English,' I explain. 'He did give me this though,' I add, handing him the invoice and necking his drink as he goes to read it. 'Ew, what the fuck is that!' I say loudly, screwing my face up as the unpleasant taste of whatever Brian was drinking assaults my palette.

He looks around the bar, mortified. 'Ricard,' he replies, giving me a very displeased look. 'The French liqueur?' he adds, observing my blank expression.

I shrug.

'Gee, must be *some* dress,' he goes on to say, giving a slight whistle as he reads the invoice. 'It's over triple the cost of the last one.'

Oh. I wonder what I've gone and ordered, then?

Having not raced to call Mother, it was inevitable that my phone would start going into erratic spasm before too long ... certainly before *I've* had the chance to go into erratic spasm myself during what is a spontaneous pre-dinner shag with Brian. What can I say, I was seduced by a second out-of-character aggressive come-on and charming Paris vibe.

'You gonna get that?' he pants.

'Well, I ... hoped it ... would ring off,' I pant back, keeping going at it.

It rings on.

'Still not ringing off,' he remarks, now straight-faced as his head slams off the massive, posh headboard.

Ugh, sod off Brian, I'm almost there!

'Who is it?' he badgers, his out-of-character, horny sex bomb head quickly falling off before his annoying business head spawns and wiggles itself back on in place of it.

I'm well aware without even needing look that it's she who must not be named during pleasures of the flesh! Or indeed at any time when one should wish to remain in a cheerful disposition.

'Could be something urgent, babe. Might be work.'

'Ugh! It's just bloody Mother, okay?!' I snap, giving up and dismounting him in a huff. 'And it's never urgent. She's probably calling me to tell me Uncle Gerald has had his fucking piles cut out.'

Well, *that's* gone and knackered it! Here I am, trying to save my wilting sex life and the thought of Uncle Gerald's arsehole has just completely killed it.

'What?!' I snap, picking up the phone.

'Oh, now that's no way to greet your mother!' she shrills. 'Not when I went to all that trouble to push you out! Anyhow, shall we do the Face-Time, dear? I want your opinion on these wedding shoes.'

My opinion? Here is a woman renowned for not giving a jot about anyone else's opinion, calling me when I'm riding my fiancé to ask for my opinion. *Really?*

'Ugh, if you must ... No!' I yell in the same breath, observing I'm in the raw.

'Stop shouting! Good grief, what's the matter with you?'

'Hang on, I'll call you back,' I mutter, throwing on a bathrobe while giving deep thought to my old Sunday school teacher, Mr Godfrey, in order to cool down. Hm, think hunchback. Working! Think beginning and endless arse in high-waisted cords. Definitely working! Think ghastly nose hair. Working all the more! Think yellowing tombstone teeth. Almost! Think attic breath. BOOM! There, now I feel sufficiently dead inside.

'Well, what do you think?' comes the unique sound of Mother's voice three seconds into Face-Time.

'I don't know, all I can see is your ceiling,' I sigh.

'Oh, is it still a brilliant white? We just had

them re-painted last month.'

'Yes, Mother, it's still a brilliant white ... er, where actually are you?!'

'I'm *here*, dear!' she trills, her camera panning so that her forehead now fills the screen.

'Are you going to show me the shoes then, before one of us dies?'

'Well, I'm trying, dear. Hang on, I'll stand in front of the hallway mirror. Just a tick.'

My eyes roll to the back of my head as she bobs toward the hallway.

'Hang on, I'll just turn the phone around so you can see,' she sings. 'There! Now, what do you think, dear? Too fancy? Not fancy enough?'

'They're fine, Mother.'

'Yes, but are they fancy?'

'Yes, they're fancy!'

'Oh, good,' she purrs, turning the phone back round, her satisfied grin quickly dropping. 'Elizabeth, cover yourself up!' she shrieks, making me jump.

I peer down to find my bathrobe gaping open at the chest. Oh.

'It's not *my* fault I have boobs,' I contest, quickly moving to conceal them.

'No, but it *is* your fault they're out, dear!'

Hm, well if you do insist on calling me during adult naptime.

*****

'So, talk me through how leaving Brian quickly morphed to a weekend in Paris with him?' Brooke prompts from her desk as we sit in work on Monday morning.

'Well, I was all set to go. My bag was by the door. Then I—'

'Jumped on board the Boner Express!' she scoffs, rolling her eyes at me.

'Well, *you* weren't there to appreciate how influential he was,' I attempt by way of an explanation.

'What, someone who only humps you in missionary with the lights out on a Sunday night while you stare into space?' she challenges.

'In normal circumstances, yeah.' I shrug. 'But, God, you should have seen him! He pretty much forced himself on me. He was like an animal. He even bit my ear at one point.'

'He bit your ear?' she exclaims in surprise. 'Kinky!'

'Well, exactly!'

'So, the ear-biting was the missing piece to your Brian jigsaw?' she suggests sarcastically.

'Er, not exactly. I look at it as extra playing time. You know, to see if we might find the missing piece,' I reason.

She shoots me a look that says 'Ain't gonna happen'.

Hm.

Once Sunday night games of hide the sausage resume – which isn't long after what was obviously one-off aggressive cuddling – the sordid Dandreams reach fever pitch.

'It's happening again!' I announce, blustering out of the rain into work a fortnight on.

'The thrush came back?' Brooke guesses, looking up from her desk.

'No, you clown, not that! That's *long* sorted! Boof – death by pessary! No, I mean, the Dandreams have started again with a bloody vengeance,' I confess, switching on my computer. 'Christ, one of these days I'm going to be screaming his name out in my sleep!'

'Ah! Someone's been thinking about Mr Wonderful again!' she tuts, wagging a finger at me.

'Well, here's the thing – I haven't! I've been swamped with wedding anxiety,' I gabble back in disbelief.

'Well, your subconscious is trying to tell you

something then,' she suggests, tapping away on the keyboard in front of her.

'Don't be daft,' I dismiss, quickly opening the back door a fraction, flinging my soggy umbrella behind it, and closing it again. Well, it's easier than going to all the trouble of hanging it up to dry out.

'So, you're saying you didn't once think about getting it back on with Dan when you were making plans to leave Brian?' Brooke probes.

'No.'

'Lies!'

'Well, maybe like … *once*,' I blag, dropping onto my chair which makes a scary buckling sound under my weight. 'Fuck, I'm definitely getting heavier!' I muse out loud.

'I don't know why you don't just face facts. This is your whole problem, girl. You're in total denial,' Brooke says, taking a long sip of her oat latte.

'Well, I have packed in the Haribos now,' I tell her in my defence.

'Not with food, bonehead. Although, to be fair you probably are with that too,' she adds bluntly. 'I *meant* in terms of your love life.'

I suppose I have been treating this whole sorry situation with my love life a bit like the fridge in my old flat; knowing there's fuck-all in it, but repeatedly returning and looking in hopes that something good has just appeared by magic.

'Well, if this was all just part of some crap romance novel then I would walk away from Brian and back into Dan's arms, just like that!' I exclaim, clicking my fingers while my home screen loads. 'In fiction, there's always a good guy and a bad guy, but Brian and Dan are both good guys! And in real life it's never that simple. These airy-fairy authors skim over the crucial bits like … well, I don't know, living arrangements, careers, financial ties…' I trail off.

'Putting everyone else first,' Brooke chimes in, giving me a disapproving look.

'Controlling mothers who think the sun shines out of their son's arse,' I add.

'Their son suddenly turning into an ear-biting nympho!' Brooke sniggers.

'Nah, he's stopped with the ear biting now. We're back to crap Sunday nights again,' I tell her. 'But key to all this is that Brian is recently bereaved,' I point out, ignorant to the ringing phone beside me.

'I know. But how long can you go on playing the grief card?' she counters, looking up at me with a serious expression. 'A month? A year? A decade?'

'Oh, fuck no. I'll be *long* gone by a decade,' I half

joke.

'Really? 'Cos I can't see you ever leaving him. I can't,' she says, shaking her head sincerely. 'Er, are you gonna answer the phone?'

'I've got it!' Brooke announces later on that afternoon.

'What?' I mumble, my voice muffled somewhat by the cream bun I have my mouth around. I haven't yet found the will to get back on the dormouse diet despite the looming wedding and buckling chair.

'You think you want to leave Brian, but you can't bring yourself to do it, right?'

I nod. Evidently that's the case.

'But what if you had an excuse to leave him?' She smirks.

I pull a face. 'I can already think of umpteen but I'm still with him.'

'I mean something serious, like him cheating on you!'

'I highly doubt Brian would cheat on me, Brooke. He's too bloody boring,' I scoff, spraying the desk with remnants of cream bun.

'He's a guy, Lizzie! Most guys in relationships aren't looking to buy when they find themselves window shopping, but what if the goods were offered to him on a plate, for free? I mean, like, shit hot goods! Goods not easily turned down,' she grins, her eyes lighting up. 'Would our man Brian be strong enough to resist temptation? Or would he do business with the devil?!'

I frown. 'I don't get it?'

'A honeytrap!' she announces, clapping her hands with glee.

I look back at her, still none the wiser. 'What the fuck? Brian isn't a bee, Brooke.'

'Who said he was a bee?!'

'Well, what the fuck's a honeytrap then?' I ask, wide-eyed.

She laughs. 'It's like a sting operation! I've seen it in movies,' she explains excitedly. 'It's where you hire someone really good looking to, like, seduce someone, then they bring the evidence back to you of them being unfaithful, or not.'

Wait, people actually do this for a living?!

'Sounds like a really insane thing to do,' I point out, 'to set Brian up like that.'

'You wouldn't be setting him up, though. It's more putting him to the test! I mean, nobody's holding a gun to his head. Like, if he doesn't cheat, you know he's a truly honourable guy and …'

'Which would just make it even fucking

harder to leave him!' I groan.

'Well, you might end up not even wanting to leave him. But, if he cheats, then you know it was always in him and girl, you got yourself a get outta jail card right there!'

Before I know it, the phones are diverted and we're sat on onceuponacheat.com like a modern-day Cagney and Lacey, trawling through the profiles of various honey trappers.

'Hm, what's Brian's usual type?' Brooke asks, clicking her tongue.

'Well, me, obviously!' I reply.

'Yeah, but they're all, like, total hotties on here. None of them look like you.'

None taken.

She looks at me. 'I mean, you're an amazing person and all, but, well, they gotta be hot stuff to entice the guys, right?' she reasons.

Suddenly, I'm not sure I like the idea of Brian being around "hot stuff". I mean, yeah, I think I need to leave him, but I guess like Nick Jonas, I still get jealous.

'What about her?' Brooke suggests, pointing to the profile of a stunning blonde with a megawatt smile.

'I hate her already!' I whinge.

'You're getting emotionally invested,' Brooke

warns. 'It's not like there's going to be a real relationship between them. It's a sting, remember?! Whoever we choose is doing you a favour.'

'I know, but, well, I don't like the thought of him biting her ear, okay?' I mumble.

'If he bites her ear, he's history and those Dan-dreams you've been having become a reality. You want him to bite her fucking ear!'

I shrug.

'So, when would be a good time to do this?' Brooke asks as if we were organising a yoga class, hovering the mouse over the "Book" tab for Sapphire, the stunning blonde. 'Bearing in mind that time is not on our side here,' she quickly adds.

'I don't know, he never bloody goes anywhere except work,' I reply.

'You don't think he'd be looking to crash the custard truck while at work, then?'

'No way! Who does?!' I reply in disbelief, forgetting all those day-dreams I used to have about Dan and I in the disabled toilets at Trip Hut.

'I don't know, Hugh Hefner maybe?'

'Possibly, when he was alive, anyway,' I muse. 'But Brian's no Hugh Hefner! He rarely looks to crash the custard truck at home. This isn't going to be as easy as you think.'

'Isn't his bachelor weekend in like, two weeks?'

Brooke reminds me.

Bingo!

Most brides-to-be probably wave the groom off on their stag with a stern warning for the best man and a certain degree of trepidation, reminding them to call every so often as though this is reassurance that they're not out burying the weasel one last time, but here's me lining my groom up with a guaranteed shag! What kind of a nutcase am I?!

'I'll get this on my credit card,' Brooke says casually, like she does this sort of shit all the time. 'You don't want onceuponacheat.com listed on your bank statements.'

She's right. I am officially insane, and nobody must ever get to know about it!

Chapter 8:

Temptation

The Monday prior to Brian's stag weekend, during breakfast in the orangery, I stare across at him sat with his leg crossed over, immersed in his newspaper, and try – and fail – to imagine him getting off with the honey trapper. I peer down at his funky socks which just drive it home all the more. He's not going to touch her; not even with a rolled-up copy of the *Financial Times* sticking out of her arse! And, if he did, he'd probably be sat there doing the crossword while her saucy striptease goes unnoticed.

Brooke disagrees, such that we now have a $100 wager going between us.

Do I feel bad as I sit here across the room from Brian with him only vaguely aware of my presence behind his massive newspaper? No. I did to begin with, but now I'm more intrigued than anything. I think I know Brian, but how well? Is he truly in love with me for *me*? Is he capable of doing the dirty? It would be interesting to find out before I marry him – all a little late in the day, I know, but still. You wouldn't buy a car without carrying out the necessary background checks, and a car is just a lump of bloody metal. Guaranteed to fuck you over when it fails to start every so often, yes, but beyond that, cars seldom break your heart.

I reckon it'll actually be quite entertaining to watch. Yes, our girl Sapphire is to be wired with a mic and body cam when she arrives at the Bellagio in Vegas on Saturday to put Brian to the test, and Brooke and I are treating the viewing like the bloody Super Bowl – I mean, we have popcorn and everything.

But when all is said and done, Brooke's right. If he cheats, then it was always in him and I should definitely walk and, if he doesn't ... well, I might just find I don't want to walk after all.

As Brian's stag weekend draws nearer, I find myself at my wits end with preparations for my hen weekend for two highly significant reasons:

1. Mother has invited herself along
2. Duchess has invited herself along

The only saving grace is that it's not actually guaranteed to go ahead, what with everything wedding-related now resting on Brian not getting off with the honey trapper this weekend.

But not satisfied at having invited herself along, Duchess – according to Brooke as chief organiser – has done nothing but complain about whatever plans have been made. Anything Brooke has organised on my behalf was never likely to acquire Duchess' seal of approval, but even so, don't like it? Don't fucking come, right?! It really is as simple as that. Oh, but *not* where the she-devil is concerned …

Duchess' to-do list:

1. Invite self on hen weekend
2. Whinge about plans for hen weekend
3. Complain to Brian when advised not to come on hen weekend
4. Be satisfied but not satisfied at being assured welcome on hen weekend
5. Repeat steps 2-5 until hen weekend ruined

On the flip side, I have Mother ringing me day and night excited to the point of soiling herself about all aspects of the wedding and hen weekend. I honestly feel like cancelling everything and fucking off somewhere!

'Can I have a word?' Brooke asks me at work later on.

'Stop! Do not speak that woman's name,' I tell her firmly, my sixth sense telling me it's all kicked off again.

'But—'

'No honestly, Brooke, not a bloody word!' I insist.

She tries again, looking frustrated. 'No, you don't underst—'

'Not listening, la, la, la!'

'LOOK! STOP RECOMMEDING ONCE UPON A CHEAT TO THE FUCKING CLIENTS, WOULD YOU?' she shouts over me.

Oh, *that*.

'I've had two emails from angry grooms about it already!'

'Well, I just thought my fellow sisters had a right to know that these services are out there.' I shrug. 'Think of the broken hearts I could be sparing!'

'Hm, well how about sparing my homeless ass? 'Cos we ain't gonna be planning many weddings if our grooms keep getting nailed by honeytraps!'

Fair enough.

Later that evening, Brian breezes into the kitchen just as I'm seeing off the last of the twinkie I bought on my way home – although "seeing off" is a bit of an understatement ... practically annihilating is nearer to the truth.

'You're home early,' I remark, my words barely audible through the gob-full of twinkie.

'Should you be eating that?' he frowns, looking appalled.

'Why's that?' I challenge, spraying him with bits of it on his approach.

He pauses in thought for a moment, as though carefully finding his words.

'Honey, you're putting on weight. You've noticed that, right?'

Oh.

A brief silence follows - well, other than for the sound of my chewing and swallowing down the rest of the twinkie – as I consider my response. Hm. It's taking a while. I mean, what do you say to something like that? *Yes*, I've put weight on. I know that, it's my body! And it's not as if I'm happy about it. I don't *like* putting on weight. I don't *like* risking splitting my work trousers every time I bend over. I don't *like* eating shit food ... I love it! That's the problem. But why is it a problem for him? He's acting as though for every pound I gain a fairy drops down dead somewhere, the bastard!

'Yeah, so?' ends up being the best I can manage.

He stares back at me for a few moments. 'Well, you are what you eat,' he finally remarks.

My mouth falls open in shock. He basically called me a twinkie!

'It's just … what a sorry waste of a great figure and, well, it's not healthy, is it? Especially since we're trying for another baby,' he continues candidly.

Mate, you'll be lucky if your instrument gets to within a near inch of me now.

'I mean, what *is* this crap? You're better than this!' he says, batting away the paper bag beside me in disgust. 'You need to be eating good, nutritious food. Not just for any future pregnancy, but for yourself,' he goes on, making me feel more like I'm in an appointment with my GP than stood in the kitchen at home with my soon-to-be husband.

Theoretically, he's right. In an ideal world we would all be stick thin and living off of fucking carrots, but the world is far from ideal, I don't care all that much for veg, and Brian is not my GP!

'I'm only thinking of you,' he says, the go-to line for when you've just made someone feel like shit. 'You want to have our baby, right?' he adds, placing a hand on my shoulder.

Hmph, actually, no.

'Yes,' I squeak with a half-arsed smile to match my sincerity.

'Well then, I don't wanna see you eating this crap again,' he says in his scary CEO voice, gesturing toward the paper bag now tossed upon the kitchen floor. 'Only good, healthy food from now on, right?'

'Right,' I mutter, head down like I just flunked my performance appraisal.

In the days following my verbal warning and the start of 'only good, healthy food from now on', I've done nothing but bloody fart! I've turned into an actual human wind farm. Usually, I take myself off to the next room if I need to fart when Brian's around because he gets a bit offended, but it's a trying task when they're brewing every three to four minutes. Nobody can be expected to go to such exhausting lengths just to appease some stuffy git who takes issue with a little flatulence. So, in accordance with the well-known saying, I've been letting my wind go free wherever I may be, whether Brian likes it or not. Well, *he's* the one who insisted on all this fibre-filled fresh fruit and veg!

As I stand getting dressed for work in the bedroom, my stomach knots up, signalling yet more wind is imminent. Paying no heed to the open bedroom window as I battle with the zip on my skirt which doesn't want to play ball today, I cut one loose. It's one of those really loud, tight ones that go on for longer than you expect, such that you find yourself pausing from whatever it is you're doing to mutter 'Jesus' or similar. In my case it's 'Oh, shit!' when I observe the open window and spot the gardener's van parked outside. Praying to fuck he's nowhere near the vicinity, I edge closer toward it, craning my neck apprehensively in search of him. I should have bloody known he'd be right outside the window, looking straight up on this bright and sunny day with zero breeze.

AGGGH! I drop down to the floor to hide in what is a knee-jerk reaction – a totally pointless one, since he's already seen me. Damn, why didn't I stay back? At least then he might have assumed it was Brian. Did he definitely hear it? Christ, I can still hear it myself. Of course, he bloody heard it! Do you know, it's not even funny anymore. Why, why, *why* must these things happen to me?!

'You've got serious issues!' Brooke exclaims during work, stopping part-way through typing out an email to pull her top over her mouth and nose

'Don't blame me! I was quite happy with zero fibre in my diet. Blame Brian!' I shrug in protest.

'You'd better pray nobody comes in to pay their balance anytime soon,' she warns in a muffled voice. 'It smells like the fucking drains have gone.'

'It will do, my arse is like a Bunsen burner! I've never eaten so much fruit and veg. Haribo Strawberries is about the best it gets for me,' I huff.

'*And* a second bite at the apple with Dan!' she says with a wink. 'Don't worry, it's on the horizon, chick. Only forty-eight hours to go until Brian falls into the honeytrap.'

'Uh, could you be any more casual about it?' I scoff. 'Anyway, Dan has probably moved on by now, it's been a good few months,' I muse distantly, suddenly swathed with melancholy and hoping to God he hasn't, as though expecting him to live as a bachelor forevermore while I'm off getting hitched is a fair and reasonable expectation.

*****

Brian almost stops my heart when he mentions casually over dinner that evening that he's toying with the idea of postponing his bachelor weekend because they're about to 'strike a huge deal at work' which he really wants to be around to oversee.

'But, Brian, the business employs plenty of bright and capable people. Surely somebody else could be tasked with this. What about Howard, why can't he take care of it?' I challenge.

'Howard's not been around much lately, his health's not so good,' he counters, leaving me wondering if the shock sight of my naked hide has anything to do with it. 'Besides, most of the top-level guys will be with me on the weekender.'

'So, you're saying there's nobody else in the entire workforce capable of overseeing things? Jesus, Brian! If that's the case then you should sack everyone else and save yourself a shit tonne of cash,' I fire back.

He looks at me curiously from across the table. 'Honey, this is big stuff. How come the prospect of postponing my weekend in Vegas is such an issue for you?' he asks with a frown.

Er, because Brooke and I have gone to the trouble of arranging a honeytrap for you. At least have the common decency to show up for it!

I give a sideways glance. 'Because you're getting married, Brian! You'll only do this once.' Perhaps. 'The business comes before all else ninety-nine percent of the time. Could you not just let it take a back seat this once and go and let your hair down on your weekend away?' I argue.

He pauses in thought for a moment as I transmit telepathic commands to his subconscious through my eyes: You will go to Vegas! You will go to Vegas! You will go to Vegas!

'Okay, okay!' he relents, raising his hands in defence. 'If it'll make you happy, I'll go to Vegas as planned.'

Wow! It bloody worked!

'See you Sunday, baby,' Brian utters, one eye on my breakfast plate as he sweeps into the orangery the next morning.

Relax, man. It's just a grapefruit!

'I guess this is the part where you tell me to have fun but not too much fun, right?' he mumbles, checking his phone.

No, Brian, knock yourself out! You go and have all the fun you want.

I force a smile – not that he's even looking at me to observe it.

Casting my mind back to how we were at Christmas, I conclude he's definitely more distant since then. His patience is thinner, his remarks blunter and, as he leans over and pecks me on the lips on his way out the door, I note his kisses are decidedly briefer. I wonder if it can all be explained away as the ongoing effects of grief or, perhaps, a possibility I haven't considered until now – could he be falling out of love with me?

I guess we're about to find out.

To-do list:

1. Buy in proper snacks
2. Cleverly dispose of all evidence of existence of proper snacks (unless walking out on Brian after his infidelity, in which case, leave wrappers and packaging lying around everywhere in two-finger salute)

*****

'Woo! This place is un-fucking real,' Brooke gasps, entering through the front door with her overnight bag and a look of astonishment as we arrive home after work.

'Keep it down, the butler's still about,' I warn under my breath.

'Holy cow, the size of that staircase!' she squeals, dropping her bag heavily onto the floor *and* my toe as she races up it, her footsteps reverberating like those of a boisterous kid at some indoor play area, opposed to a supposedly mature adult.

'Ouch! Brooke, what are you doing?'

'This!' she yells back, arriving at the top and mounting the banister.

'You're not going to...' I begin.

Phew, she's not going to hump it; she's sliding

down it. Yikes!

'Be careful,' I hiss over her cheers and whoops, 'I don't fancy clearing up your splattered remains.'

'Staircases like this were made for sliding down!' she declares, plopping off the bottom. 'Oh, fuck!' she suddenly gasps, looking up at me and then down at the floor.

'What?'

'My laptop!' she pants.

'What about it?' I ask, following her finger down toward her overnight bag laying in a heap by my foot.

Luckily, we find Brooke's laptop in one piece as she ham-fistedly unpacks everything out onto the bed in one of the guest bedrooms.

'Phew, we're still good for tomorrow night's viewing entertainment!' she sighs, rubbing her hands together.

I reach into my pocket when my phone tinkles with an alert.

Brian arrived at Two Palms Hotel & Casino, Las Vegas.

'They've arrived in Vegas,' I announce, thinking how efficient these tracking apps are and the possibilities there could be if there was one that could tell you exactly what any random person is up to.

Brian just committed adultery, Las Vegas.

Dan Elliott just thought about you, London.

Duchess is placing pins in her voodoo doll of you, Newark, US.

Actually, it's a blessing that this isn't a thing, I think to myself, picturing the sort of data it would have on me.

Lizzie ate nine Maryland cookies, Two's Company, NY city.

Lizzie is slagging off Brian, Two's Company, NY city.

Lizzie just pissed in the shower, Home.

Hm.

'Showtime!' Brooke exclaims, her grin quickly dropping. 'Hey, is this place haunted? I keep seeing shadows out the corner of my eye.'

'No, that'll be the butler,' I shout, directing my voice out toward the hallway in hope that the nosey shit heard.

Having largely lived off of wholesome foodstuffs under Brian's watchful eye for the past week, the prospect of pizza – strictly off Brian's and the butler's watch – was one I was very much looking forward to, until…

'Here you go. I'm afraid it's a little caught,' Brooke warns, placing it down hesitantly on the coffee table.

'Caught? Looks more like it's been held hostage and interrogated!' I reply, observing the very sorry-looking deep-pan Hawaiian that Brooke has managed to quickly burn the arse off. 'I thought you said that you and machinery have a mutual understanding now?'

She shrugs. 'Well, I thought we did, but obviously not where Brian's big-ass cooker is concerned.'

'Great. Now what are we going to eat for dinner?'

'Well, we'll just rustle up something from the pantry,' she suggests, pulling a face as though I missed a trick.

I sigh. 'Two things. One – there's nothing worth eating in the pantry since the whole place is a trans-fat and sugar-free zone, hence the need to buy in the pizza you just cremated. And two – the lack of mutual understanding with Brian's big-arse cooker.'

'Oh, yeah. Then why don't we just order take-out?'

I emit a longer sigh. 'Because, unfortunately, the person delivering said take-out would have a starring role in Brian's round-the-clock CCTV show, which, let's face it, he's probably watching from his phone in Vegas,' I scoff. 'Then I'll be in line for another bloody verbal about eating crap!'

'Jeez, Lizzie, when you said you liked a little domination I thought you meant in the sack!' Brooke gasps in disbelief. 'This isn't right or healthy, Brian telling you what you can and can't eat. You're not a fricking toddler! What's he gonna do next, tell you when to go to bed?'

She observes my guilty glance.

'Oh, gee! He does that too?!' she asks, astounded.

'Sometimes.'

'Right, that's it!' she says, unlocking her phone.

'You're not ringing him?!' I explode in panic.

'No, I'm ordering us the biggest fucking pizza they do!' she replies. 'And if Brian's got anything to say about it, he can say it to me, because I'll give him some food for thought and it won't be fucking wholesome!'

Feisty!

As Saturday morning dawns, I wake in two minds:

Mind one: *Tonight's the night! Brian is going to do the dirty with that walking Barbie doll!*

Mind two: *Tonight's the night! Brian had better*

not do the dirty with that walking Barbie doll!

I've spent all this time looking for a way out of my relationship, but now as I'm faced with the prospect of being cheated on at my own doing, I'm not so sure about things.

'Your breakfast is out on the table, ma'am. Chia seeds and berries as Mr Garcia requested on your behalf,' the butler greets me as I descend the staircase.

What?! Ah, fuck it, I hope he shags her into next week!

'Your house guest is arranging her own ... breakfast,' he adds, giving me a strange look.

I discover the reason behind the look when I walk into the kitchen to find it in a state akin to a bombed bakery; eggs and flour everywhere with Brooke standing in amongst it all looking like a slovenly Geisha.

'Hey! Do you know how to stop pancakes from sticking to the pan?' she asks, sheepishly holding up a blackened frying pan with an incinerated pancake stuck to the arse of it.

I stare back at her. The last time I tampered with eggs, I was still finding bits of them all over my flat for a week. I'm *not* the person to ask!

With the butler kept busy clearing up the car crash in the kitchen, we discuss arrangements for tonight's secret sting operation.

'So, Brian definitely said they were planning to eat around 7pm, then go on to the bar, then onto the casino, right?' Brooke asks with her detective head on.

'Yeah, that's what he said in his text this morning,' I reply.

'Okay, I'll text Sapphire to tell her to be in the bar for after 9pm then,' she says. 'That ought to give them enough time to get dinner done and be in the bar for when she walks in so Brian spots her from the off.'

I nod, probably a little too despondently.

'Don't be a dick!' Brooke groans, sensing my jealousy. 'Brian ain't the one! If he was, he wouldn't give a shit about your size.'

Is it true? Is Brian only interested in slinky blondes?

'What if he really was just thinking about my health, though?' I challenge.

'He wasn't, Lizzie! He was just thinking about how it'll look, some high-flying CEO like him with anything more than a size six on his arm!' she counters. 'Brian has only known you at your physical best, remember? Whereas Dan knew you at your worst and wanted you for *you*, not the way you looked.'

Hm. I never had Brian down as the shallow type, but then nor did I have him down as the

Hitler type – which he is. So, what do I know?

The show must go on!

*****

'Anything happening yet?' Brooke calls out from the kitchen.

'No, still just a black screen,' I shout back from behind Brooke's laptop in the front room.

Hands trembling, I reach for my vodka and orange, taking an ultra-long sip. Why am I this nervous? My heart is literally pounding in my ears! Perhaps it's because the future rests on whatever happens tonight – I'm going to be forced to make a decision about my relationship with Brian one way or another. *God*, I hope it's the right one!

'Here we go, screw you, Brian!' Brooke cackles, placing the popcorn, potato chips and tub of Ben and Jerry's she brought with her over on the table.

'Damn, I've missed you!' I whisper, making a desperate lunge for the ice cream before all else. Uh! What luxury just to be eating it with an actual spoon.

Suddenly, movement on the laptop screen grabs my attention. A grainy image of sumptuously plush bar-like surroundings comes in and out of focus.

'We're on!' I shout, half choking on a mouthful of cookie dough.

'Oh-my-God-oh-my-God!' Brooke squeals, diving onto the sofa beside me.

There comes the hiss and crackle of some audio interference before a silky voice asks, 'Hello, can you hear me alright?'

'Loud and clear!' Brooke calls back through the laptop mic.

'Okay, I'm just walking into the bar now. There's a table of guys to my right, is that them?' Sapphire asks under her breath, turning slightly toward them.

I instantly spot Brian sat at the table, his wild arm gesticulation no doubt being accompanied by several business buzzwords.

'Yeah, that's them!'

'Okay and which is Brian?'

'He's the one wearing the blue shirt,' I reply around another mouthful of ice cream.

'There's two guys in blue shirts,' Sapphire quickly points out.

'Ah. He's the one sitting closest to you,' I advise. 'If in doubt, just look for fluorescent stripey socks.'

'Ah, hang on,' she says, the camera dipping slightly as she ducks to look under the table.

'Yeah, I see the socks.'

We emit a simultaneous snort of laughter as she proceeds to walk slowly past their table. All heads turn but Brian's, whose CEO-like voice is vaguely audible as she passes.

'I mean, it's a massive leap versus last fiscal year,' we hear him say.

Oh my God! Who actually does business talks on their bachelor party weekend?

'Looks like you should have that hundred bucks at the ready,' I warn Brooke, rolling my eyes.

Sapphire makes her way over to the bar where she orders a Screaming Orgasm in a husky tone and perches on a bar stool.

'Just gonna unbutton my top a little,' she whispers down the mic.

'Wowzas! She's even turning *me* on!' Brooke mumbles. 'If Brian doesn't go for this, I'll be damned!'

'You will be!' I scoff.

The camera pans around as Sapphire spins on the stool to face Brian's table. After several minutes of nothing, and just as I find myself waking with a jolt from a ten-second nap, Brian comes into view on his way over toward the bar.

'And action, baby!' Brooke yells, springing up

from the sofa and kicking my drink over on the coffee table, leaving me watching in open-mouthed in horror as the laptop dies a slow death by vodka and orange.

'Whoops, shit.'

'You idiot! Quick, do something!' I yell as we both bluster about in panic like headless chickens.

'Like what? The screen's gone all funny,' she wails, tapping the keys desperately.

'Well, I don't know, can we view it on our phones?' I ask.

'That might work, but I don't know the URL to the live stream,' she replies. 'It was saved on the laptop.'

'Did you save it anywhere else?'

'Well, I did have it on an email, but I deleted that, you know, to get rid of the evidence,' she reveals with an accomplished grin, as though I should be impressed with her forward thinking.

'But there's more chance you plaiting your own piss than Brian ever checking your emails!' I argue, my eyes rolling to the back of my head.

'Ah, yeah,' she agrees, staring at the screen.

'Great. That's *that* knackered then!' I sigh on my way through to the kitchen for a cloth.

'Chill! I can just text Sapphire later, she'll tell

us how it went,' Brooke says, following me.

I needed him to tell me, though. To see what he did. What he said. How he acted around her. It would have told me all I needed to know.

*****

Most would be happier than Pharrell Williams to learn that their soon-to-be spouse didn't cop off with the honeytrap on their bachelor party weekender. But then again, most wouldn't be organising honeytraps in the first bloody place! Brian's only offence, as it later transpires, was buying Sapphire a Screaming Orgasm which can't really be deemed a crime when compared to giving her one. It *is* in my book, just not up there with justifications for giving up on your relationship. Of course, it would have told me a lot about how he really feels about me to have seen for myself exactly how he behaved. It's never hard to spot when your man's noticed a chick he likes the look of. Call it a woman's intuition, but us girls know the dead giveaways, including, but not limited to:

1. **Posture**: Suddenly taller. Head bolt upright in manner of horny cockerel. Arms overly out to side giving illusion of burly physique.
2. **Expression**: Deadly serious and/or far away, as though this signals he has not noticed/is not checking out other fe-

male.
3. **Eyes**: Looking around innocently, then quickly reverting back in direction of other female, and repeat. Often accompanied by casual whistle.
4. **Voice**: Suddenly louder and deeper. Often accompanied by fake cough.
5. **Cash**: Splashing of.
6. **Humour**: Sudden acquisition of.

We already know Brian is guilty of item five, since he bought Sapphire a drink. Why, though? Why buy a total stranger a drink? It's obvious why – the git was flirting! Some women don't bat an eyelid and write it off as human nature. Well, call me old fashioned, but I want to be the only woman to exist in the eyes of my husband – whether or not I lie in bed beside him at night having filthy dreams about Dan Elliott, which are totally involuntary and therefore irrelevant, by the way.

I spend the best part of Sunday busier than a mosquito at an orgy getting rid of all evidence of my insubordinate food bender, violently tossing bottles and packets into a bin liner and talking to myself as I go.

'So, he wants to buy other women Screaming Orgasms, does he? Hmph! See if I care!'

Hearing car wheels out on the gravel in the

late afternoon, I find myself needing to remember my breathing as part of me gears up to pounce like a Rottweiler and tear a strip off him.

'How'd the weekend go? Enjoy yourself, did you?' I ask, my tone almost giving me away as he blusters in through the front door with his bags.

'Hey, honey!' he smiles, greeting me with the usual brief peck. 'Yeah, great fun.'

Hmph! Playing with Barbie dolls always *is*.

'Glad to be home, though. Good to get back to business, you know?'

Oh, not to me, then?

'I'm gonna go freshen up and check my emails,' he says, disappearing off up the stairs without another word, leaving me swathed in suspicion.

He's definitely off with me. Is it guilt? Was there more to that Screaming Orgasm than Sapphire is letting on? I can't very well ask him, can I?

Ugh! This weekend was supposed to give me answers, but all its done is give me more bloody questions! I'm in a worse position than I was before and meanwhile, the wedding is drawing closer and closer. Now I don't know *what* the hell to do.

Chapter 9:

Here Come the Girls!

The following weekend, I find both my head and arse in the clouds on a plane heading for London. No, I haven't finally grown some balls and left Brian. I'm going on my hen weekend; the hen weekend I had hoped may not go ahead, but somehow *is*.

Alongside Brooke and I are Melodie and Jen, both former Wilson Garcia colleagues, Monica, the sandwich delivery girl from work, wedding photographer Laura, and someone who needs no introductions … Duchess. Although, quite what she's doing here is anyone's guess, what with her having dissented with the majority on all aspects of the planning. Call it a hunch but I imagine the only purpose of the cow's presence is to keep a reptilian eye firmly on me.

Now here we all are, sat on the plane feeling awkward as arse. Nobody dares speak in case of a blasphemous slip of the tongue, limiting us to careful small talk about what the white plastic "table thingies" in takeaway pizzas are actually for and other such wonders of the world. How the hell are we to cope five thousand miles away in London with *her* tagging along, giving us daggers, rolling her eyes at everything, bitching, moaning, and complaining? I'll be watching my back constantly knowing she's reporting everything back to US HQ before you can say "pre-marital domestic". It would all have been so convenient if she and Mother got on. They could have whiled away the afternoons bitching over afternoon tea at Claridge's. Sigh.

Some bloody hen weekend *this* is set to be.

Hours later, just when I think things can't get any worse, I spot Mother waving erratically in arrivals wearing a corduroy Baker Boy hat and an insane grin. Hold up, what the fuck is that?! Bugger me, she's only wearing a bum-bag! The hat's bad enough all by itself but why the fuck did she go and add to it with that monstrosity?! I can tell just from her expression that this is the exciting weekend away with the Girl Guides she never had, but if I know Brooke at all well then I imagine Mother's in for a bloody shock.

'Coooey!' she yells, her ear-splitting shrill turning heads all around us. 'I'm over here, dear!'

As if she wasn't easily spotted in *that* ensemble.

'How are you, dear? Good flight?' she asks, before immediately launching into an extraordinarily detailed account of everything she's packed for the weekend while we all stand gawking at her wondering when it's going to stop.

'Oh, you haven't introduced me to your girlfriends, dear!' she eventually exclaims, patting down her hair.

You didn't give me the fucking chance!

With introductions eventually done – along with the frosty, unenthusiastic reacquaintance of Mother and Duchess – we locate our minibus driver from the cordon of expressionless faces holding up signs outside arrivals. Ours is a short and portly chap holding up a piece of card displaying Brooke's name – missing the 'e' – in scruffy marker pen.

'Awight darlin'? You Bwook, are ya?' he greets me, surveying all of us bar Mother and Duchess from top to bottom.

'No, I'm Lizzie. Bwook booked it, she's over there,' I smirk, pointing her out.

"Ello, the guv didn't tell me I was gettin' an 'en party!' he remarks, his eyes lighting up as he spies the t-shirts Brooke had made for us, with only Duchess point-blank refusing to wear one. 'You gals just be'ave yaselves, know what I mean?' He winks, earning himself a couple of death stares from the gruesome twosome.

I find myself pulling code faces in Brooke's direction and lagging behind as we follow him out to our transport.

'Something in your eye?' she asks, completely oblivious.

'Ugh, no. Dan works here, remember?' I mumble discreetly.

'Oh yeah!' she more or less shouts, prompting everyone in front to turn around.

I shush her under my breath. 'Keep your voice down and your eyes peeled!', I say, scanning the vicinity for any sign of those guns and that arse. Nope, nothing. The only thing to be observed is Mother's arse busy manhandling my adult guests into an orderly line to board the minibus. Ye Gods, she's at it already!

'Which one of yous is the bwide, then?' the driver asks, clambering inside and plonking his tubby mass heavily into his seat, causing the minibus to wobble from side to side.

'I don't think I care for his standard of grammar,' Mother mutters in the seat behind me.

'Oh, that'll be me,' I tell him, raising my hand in a manner significantly lacking the excitable buzz of any usual bride-to-be embarking upon her hen weekend.

I observe his piggy eyes ogling me through the interior mirror. 'Well, if I was ten years younger,' he sighs, before pulling away at breakneck speed, making our heads jerk violently.

Pfft! Ten years younger? He'd need to be totally reborn as someone else!

Eventually, we pull up outside our hotel in Mayfair, putting an end to the driver's unwelcome flirty banter as well as Mother's endless tallying of Eddie Stobart lorries.

'Right, let's check in, unpack and all meet in the lounge for a lovely, refreshing cup of tea,' she booms across the hotel foyer.

'You can if you like, but we're going up to our rooms to order room service and have a kip,' I tell her, swiping the grin straight off her face.

'You can't go using words like kip in an establishment like this,' she mutters through clenched teeth, ducking behind my shoulder and peering about the place in panic as though she doesn't already look a tit in that ridiculous hat and bumbag combo.

'Good idea, we gotta preserve some energy for hitting the clubs tonight,' Brooke adds with a wink, leaving Mother's mouth hanging open and Duchess battling to scowl through all the Botox.

'Darling, we're in a five-star luxury London spa hotel, surely it would be an idea to make use of the spa?' she suggests in a slow, mocking tone.

'Yes, we'll get a facial before we head out,'

Brooke replies, giving her a firm slap on the back and leaving her gobsmacked.

When loud, incessant knocking comes at the door to Brooke, Monica, and my room later that afternoon, I know immediately it's not room service. Only one person in this world has the audacity to knock in such a manner.

'It's your mom,' Monica confirms, squinting through the spyhole.

Sigh.

'Quick, hide the booze or we'll never hear the end of it!' I gasp, springing up off the bed and rushing to hide the collection of duty-free spirits resting upon the dressing table and the lipstick-stained coffee cups we were forced to drink from with no glasses to hand.

'But I'm thirty-two!' Monica contests with wide eyes.

'I realise that, but trust me, it's easier all round if we just hide them,' I warn, feeling a tit.

She nods half-heartedly, beginning to open the door and almost falling over as Mother blusters in before it's even fully opened.

'Now, why did they go and put you in a room two floors away from mine?!' she demands, mopping her fevered brow with a floral handkerchief. 'It's ridiculous, it really is. I've had quite a trek!'

'Because that's all they had,' I lie through my teeth, observing Brooke's and Monica's smirks out the corner of my eye as Mother rushes to check her appearance in the mirror.

'Well, it's most inconvenient,' she mutters, giving her hair a zhoosh. 'Now, whilst I have your attention, I'd like to go over the itinerary for this evening,' she announces, as though she has any say in the matter.

*****

'Well, I don't think Daddy would be at all happy to learn that I'm out frolicking in nightclubs, dear,' Mother complains over dinner, her bottom lip practically hanging down into her chicken chasseur.

My sentiments waver between two schools of thought:

1. I'm certain Dad couldn't actually give a fuck.
2. What else did she expect a bunch of women our age to be doing on a hen weekend?

'Well, stay here by yourself then,' I suggest coolly.

Her head shoots up. 'You're not planning to abandon me here at the hotel all by myself, surely?' she pleads with cow eyes normally reserved for the rare occasions Dad finds the balls to stand firm.

'No,' I reply, observing her expression lifting somewhat, 'you'll have Veronica to keep you company.'

Duchess almost chokes on a piece of tenderstem broccoli as Mother's faces falls in horror.

'What time do we leave?' Mother bellows across the table, making everyone jump out their skins.

Later, with the cocktails flowing during our Mayfair bar crawl, Mother already over at the bar demanding they turn the music down, and Duchess's capacity to earwig into our conversation conveniently compromised, Brooke hesitantly pulls me to one side, her guilty expression demonstrative that a bombshell may be imminent.

'So, it was meant to be a surprise, bit of a last-minute thing between us girls, but I'm thinking you should know we've organised a male stripper to come to the club tonight,' she enlightens me. 'His name's Fabio, he's Italian and he's hung like a donkey, supposedly.'

I almost choke on my Cosmopolitan. 'Please tell me you're joking!' I plead.

She shakes her head. 'We thought you might like to see some guns one last time before you marry Brian, who doesn't have any.'

Hm, can't argue with that, but there are two not-so-small issues with this. Glancing over at said issues, I observe Mother now perched at the end of our booth looking very out of place and the polar opposite to the words displayed on her hen party sash. Pfft! "Hot Mama"? "Big Baby" is more like it. Then there's Duchess sat in the middle with her contrasting streaked bouffant and edgy black leather blazer, grimacing like an angry badger.

'Sorry if it's taking a while to speak,' I reply through clenched teeth after a long pause. 'I'm just picturing their reactions when some guy rocks up waving his tackle about! Are you out of your mind, woman?!'

'Oh, they'll come around,' she dismisses. 'All the old chicks love a bit of young pecker.'

'And you know this how?' I gasp, staring at her dumbfoundedly as her straw hits the bottom of her cocktail glass and she deliberately sits slurping at nothing while she considers her response.

'Oh, chill out, Lizzie! They'll be the ones screaming the loudest, trust me,' she replies eventually.

'Yeah, screaming at *me*!' I huff, my mind going ten to the dozen trying to think of ways to get rid of them before Fabio rocks up at the club. Hm ... If we could only lose them along the way. Well, it worked with Hansel and Gretel?! Doh, no good. Not gutsy enough and swathed in guilt already!

'You need to get on the phone and cancel this Fabio, now!' I demand.

'I can't, it's out of business hours and you have to give, like, proper notice to the agency. It's too late.' Brooke shrugs. 'Besides, it's all paid for, so I say we just roll with it and have a bit of fun. That's what bachelorette parties are all about, Lizzie, jeez! Relax.'

Okay, so there's really only one thing for it: get them both pissed out of their skulls in hopes they'll wake tomorrow with little recollection of any young Italian with his knob out!

'How long have we got?' I ask in desperation.

'Just under an hour 'til we need to leave for the club,' Brooke replies, glancing at her watch.

And with that, Operation Giggle Juice is launched. Tequilas all round. Mother is easily talked into participating with made up tales of how the Queen herself has three or four each evening to relax and unwind. Duchess is harder to convince and sticks to the single cocktail she's made last the night thus far.

'Right girls, we gotta head off,' Brooke announces a little under an hour later.

'Oh? Aren't we going to have more of those slammer things?' Mother asks disappointedly, her eyes appearing more glazed and bloodshot by the second.

'Oh, don't worry, they got slammers at the club,' Brooke smirks, giving me a discreet thumbs-up.

'Oh, good!' Mother squeaks, hauling herself up out of the booth, linking Melodie's arm and practically skipping her way there.

'What we gonna do about Shitface?' Brooke asks bluntly, gesturing toward a barely tipsy Duchess striding huffily well ahead, her designer kitten heels aggressively clip-clopping the pavement.

'Dunno,' I sigh, 'and the more booze I have, the less I bloody care!'

'Like your thinking!' Brooke grins, slinging an arm around me as we head off into the slightly chilly but buzzing evening air.

Minutes later, by an amazing stroke of luck, Duchess resolves the problem of her festering presence all by herself when she opts to hail a cab and fuck off back to the hotel, muttering something about a headache as she clambers in and disappears off down the street. Good bloody riddance! That just leaves Mother, which is bad enough, but by the looks of it she shouldn't be too much of a problem now she's suitably pissed.

The former statement is immediately called

into question around half an hour and two further tequila slammers later when the infamous Fabio slinks over, mounts our table and begins gyrating in our faces, sending Mother into a bigger frenzy than any of us.

'Show us your sausage!' she screeches, her eyes out on stalks as he strips down to a flimsy red G-string. 'Come on! What are you piddling about for? Get it off, man!' she roars, slapping his arse so hard he almost falls off the table.

'Please, no touch!' he winces, rubbing at his inflamed buttock.

I cover my eyes with my hen party sash, cringing like hell.

'By Jove, what firm buns he has!' she beams, clapping her hands delightedly.

'Evening!' I nod awkwardly toward the various club patrons passing by our table, pointing open-mouthed at Fabio and then at Mother who is completely off her tits and out of control.

Fabio suddenly grasps my head with both his hands and forces it into his thrusting crotch.

'Help!' I squeak, my voice muffled by his package.

Well, what am I supposed to do? How do you even respond to *that*?! Particularly with a no touching rule in place. Praying that, unlike me, he's not of a windy disposition, I duck below his open legs in front of me and shoot Brooke a look of horror across the table. Quite how I didn't guess her attention would be completely transfixed on Fabio's muscley buttocks – one of them possibly now sporting Mother's angry pink handprint – I *don't* know.

'No touch! No touch!' Fabio warns repeatedly as Mother makes a cross-eyed lunge for his tackle.

'Oh, stop it you, big tease!' she slurs. 'Any man who puts himself in this line of work shouldn't be shy with his manhood!'

Jesus Christ! I'm not sure what's bloody worse, disapproving Mother or slutty, promiscuous Mother! I decide on slutty, promiscuous Mother at the point Fabio finally whips off his thong, causing her to screech like a pterodactyl.

'Good golly! It's double the size of your father's!' she roars, making me very nearly vomit in my mouth.

*****

Missing:

Woman, late fifties, wearing navy twin set and pearls.

Last seen in conga line at Sensations Nightclub sometime between 1am and 2am.

Ugh. How typical of Mother to go AWOL after I'd needed her to the most. She's always got to be bloody awkward.

'I've checked the Ladies for, like, the fifth time now, but she's nowhere to be seen,' Brooke says with a shrug.

'Okay, I'm going to go and ask the DJ to put out an announcement over the mic,' I announce, growing worried on my way over to the booth. Not just for Mother's welfare, but for how it's going to sound in this trendy London nightclub when the DJ kills the music to request that Petunia Bradshaw make her way to the stage and, even worse, how it's going to look if she does, pissed out of her bleeding skull at her age!

I'm almost relieved when she doesn't show up, yet simultaneously worried sick that she hasn't. Where the hell is she?! We've covered every square foot of the club but she's nowhere to be seen. The only thing to assume is that she left the club unnoticed.

'Last I saw she was running after Fabio asking if he'd be interested in a summer season at the country club or something,' Laura recalls.

What the...? I sincerely hope he didn't oblige, for her sake. She'll be bloody mortified when she sobers up!

'That must've been at least a couple hours ago. I saw her dancing after that,' Jen adds.

'Did anyone see her leave the dancefloor?' I ask, anxiously.

The girls shake their heads in unison.

'Oh my God, I'm the worst daughter in the world!' I wail over the pumping bass, burying my face in my hands and suddenly feeling very sober from all the worry.

'No, you're not. It's your bachelorette. It's not down to you to babysit everyone, we're all responsible adults,' Monica chimes in. A point which would otherwise have been valid had Brooke and I not plied Mother with tequila.

'Even so, what are we going to do?' I plead, beginning to well up as scenes of the worst scenarios play out in my mind.

'Well, she's definitely not here, we've checked everywhere,' Melodie reasons.

'I say we leave and take the search outside,' Brooke suggests.

We nod in tandem, following her out of the club and onto the progressively quietening street where there's no sign of Mother in the immediate vicinity. I had hoped she'd be parked on a bench somewhere sobering up, but no. Nothing.

'Somebody call the hotel and ask if they can check if she's there. She may have taken a cab back by herself,' Laura suggests.

'I'll do it. I have the number saved in my contacts,' Brook replies, fishing her phone out of her bag.

'Don't worry, she probably got tired, had enough and decided to slip off so as not to bother you,' Monica soothes, patting my arm.

Bless her, she can't have been in Mother's company long enough to appreciate first-hand that this would be totally out of character for someone who makes it her business to bother me.

'Well? Is she there?' I ask as Brooke hangs up the call minutes later.

'She's not in her room and they haven't seen her.' Brooke shrugs, the concern etched on her face yet more confirmation that I should be worried.

'She can't have gone far,' Jen soothes, her attempts at reassurance disappearing straight over my head.

What if she's lost? Lying hurt somewhere? Abducted, even? Well, you never know! Although I'm sure anyone abducting Mother would happily let her go in all of two minutes once they realise what a pain in the arse she is. Jokes aside, time's getting on and we have to find her!

'Hey, I thought I heard movement in the alley behind us,' Laura announces, pointing toward it hopefully.

'Okay, let's check it out, all of us together,' Brooke suggests. 'Safety in numbers, you know?'

Tentatively, we creep toward the entrance of the darkened alley.

Brooke turns on the flashlight on her phone, shining it down the passageway and straight onto some neanderthal of a bloke taking a leak. We all jump with one simultaneous gasp.

'OI! Do you bloody mind?!' he calls out in a gruff, pissed-off tone, rushing to cover himself.

Great, no sign of Mother but we have now seen our second todger of the evening!

'Now, what?' I sigh, wondering if it's time to call either Dad or the Old Bill. Or both.

'Let's give it a little bit longer, walk the area and make doubly sure she's not still around,' Melodie suggests.

We make our way down the street, a rabble of clicking heels and anxious whispers, scouring the area for any sign of Mother.

'There can't be many places left open, it's getting really late,' I puff, pulling my cropped jacket tighter around me as the night air bites.

I spy a fox eagerly devouring the remnants of a discarded kebab over by some rubbish bins, just another worrisome confirmation of how late it is.

'There's some lights a little further down. Let's go check it out. There may be a night café open or something,' Monica suggests.

'Yeah, I guess she could've gone off to grab a coffee,' Jen agrees.

The faint din of music grows progressively louder as we near the lights coming from a small, seedy-looking karaoke bar, seemingly still in full swing and possibly breaking its licence – if it has one.

'Jesus, strangled cat, much?!' Jen remarks on our approach as a God-awful rendition of Queen's "Bohemian Rhapsody" rings out.

'Is there any point checking inside?' Melodie frowns doubtfully.

I stand rooted to the spot, realisation slowly dawning that the caterwaul assaulting our ears sounds strangely familiar:

It can't be, can it?!

Reluctantly, I push open the door just as Brian May's infamous guitar solo rings out. I blink and then blink again as I spot Mother straight away, stumbling about the place steaming drunk and playing air guitar.

Chuff me, she's alive!

Taxi for the songbird.

Chapter 10:

Balls to it!

As the later part of Saturday morning dawns, I wake to a daunting recollection of last night and a text from Brian:

Hey. Mom called. Pretty upset. She's feeling left out. Please try to include her more. She's made a lot of effort to be there. Call you later. B x

What?!

'Hey! What's with all the gasping sounds?' Brooke groans from somewhere beneath a mound of duvet to my right. 'Not *another* pornographic dream about you-know-who?!'

Too pissed off to talk, I lean across to her bed, brandishing my phone in her face and somehow resisting the overwhelming urge to throw it across the room.

She frowns, squinting her mascara-encrusted eyes to read it. 'Oof!' she winces.

'Can you believe it? Can you bloody believe it? Calling herself a cab for a supposed headache and the whole time she was running off to tell tales on us! Playing the victim, feeding Brian a load of bullshit!' I snort, furiously. 'That bloody woman has issues. She's been hellbent on fucking this weekend up from day one,' I explode, my rant waking Monica who sits up rubbing her eyes confusedly. 'I mean, sitting there with a face like an angry wasp, scowling and rolling her eyes the whole time, making zero effort to fit in or engage with us, yet *we* are supposedly the bad guys!'

'Well, yeah. I mean, you should see some of the pics from the earlier part of the night,' Brooke chimes in, fetching her phone off the side table and scrolling through it. 'We're just smiley and normal and she looks all pissed off like those people in old black and white photographs.'

'Pfft! Look at her trying to be all old Hollywood,' I scoff, craning my neck to get a closer look.

'But she's just old!' Brooke giggles.

'And look at those eyebrows! I know perfect symmetry is out of the question, but bugger me!' I grimace.

'I know, right? They say to look at the brows as sisters, not twins, but *those* aren't even fucking related!'

'It only gets worse once you're married, you know that right?' Monica calls out from across the room. 'I think this is supposed to be, like, the charm offensive period.'

'Well, I think I can safely say it's been pure offense and no charm whatsoever!' I huff, flinging back the duvet and practically stomping to the wardrobe to fetch some clothes.

'Don't wear anything nice!' Brooke booms across the room.

I stop and turn to look at her. 'Sorry?!'

'Remember I told you to bring an old tracksuit?' she adds, a peculiar expression etching its way across her face.

'Yeah, and?'

'Well, you need to wear that this morning for the … activity we'll be doing.'

'I don't think I like that pause,' I remark, my usually spot-on sixth sense sensing something dodgy on the horizon.

'Can't tell you anything more at this stage. Just know that Duchess is about to be brought to justice,' Brooke adds, a wry grin creeping its way up her face.

*****

'Paintballing?!' I hiss in horror under my breath, almost choking on a mouthful of Cumberland sausage at the breakfast table.

Brooke nods. 'There, you got it out of me. Happy now?'

Hardly!

'B-but…' I stammer, gobsmacked, as I observe Mother hanging out of her arse and hunched over a bowl of muesli while Duchess nibbles toast and conserves with her snooty nose in the air.

'Relax! This is set to be the funniest day of your life,' Brooke sniggers discreetly.

*****

'Please tell me this buffoon has taken the wrong turning,' Mother groans from the back seat of the minibus upon observing the giant "Riot Paintballing" welcome sign at the leafy, wooded entrance to the site.

'Paintballing? You can't be serious!' Duchess pipes up.

'All shall be revealed,' Brooke teases as we arrive outside the reception hut and disembark the minibus.

'Well, if you think I'm taking part in some ghastly, alpha-male hurly-burly, you've another thing coming!' Duchess growls, exiting the vehicle in Versace loungewear. 'When you told us to bring a tracksuit, I assumed it would be for a spa day!'

'Hey, there's more to life than lounging around getting your ass pampered. Live a little!' Brooke fires back at her, rendering her momentarily speechless.

'Well, I think I can safely say that paintballing is not my idea of living, so kindly count me out,' Duchess barks, folding her arms in defiance like a stroppy five-year-old.

'No, no, I won't hear of it. Everyone's taking part. Brian made it very clear he doesn't want you left out and we assured him you wouldn't be,' Brooke counters firmly, draping an arm around her shoulders and practically marching her toward reception while I struggle to stifle my giggles behind my hand.

'And I hope you're not expecting me to take part in this guff!' Mother scoffs, pulling me aside by my arm.

I shrug. 'Don't blame me, I didn't book it.'

'Well, it's ridiculous! I am in no fit state for this malarky,' she argues.

'Oh, don't you bloody start as well!' I groan, rolling my eyes in exasperation. 'Anyway, this is nothing compared to *your* malarky last night! Now, you don't want me to call Dad and have him come collect you, do you? Because then I'll have to tell him all about Fabio an—'

'Alright, alright! Where do you want me?'

Ha!

'Morning, ladies. Welcome to Riot. I'm Steve,'

the scary, bald-headed, burly chap at reception greets us in a gruff, military tone. 'Grab your overalls from the box over there, masks are here on the counter.'

Duchess stands rooted to the spot in horror.

'Something the matter?' he frowns at her.

'Er … Er, no,' she squeaks, trundling zombie-like over toward the overall box, her horrid face a picture.

'Okay, outside in two minutes for briefing, please,' he orders, glancing at his watch and swiping a clipboard off the side before breezing out the door.

I daren't look in Brooke's direction as the gruesome twosome stand quiet as mice with faces like thunder, reluctantly donning their overalls as the rest of the girls chatter in excited anticipation.

I have no idea how I'm going to get through the next two hours without pissing myself!

'Okay, how many of you have been paintballing before?' Steve asks as we huddle around outside for our pre-session briefing.

No one moves, our guns dangling at our sides.

'None of you? That's okay, it's all pretty straightforward, nothing to it,' he says, cool as you like.

'Hmph, for him, maybe!' Duchess scoffs under her breath.

'Okay, this here is your gun,' he announces, holding one up demonstration. 'When you pull the trigger here, it'll fire paint balls at a speed of up to ninety metres a second toward the enemy. Obviously you're going to feel it when you get hit but it's not what I would call painful.'

Don't laugh. Don't laugh. Don't laugh.

'Now, a couple of you are looking a bit spooked, but let me tell you, it's all great fun,' he goes on. 'It's safe. The rules are simple and straightforward, and anyone can play, you don't need to have any special skills or training. Okay, you ladies will be the red team, identifiable by this red band I'm now passing round which goes around your upper arm. Your opponents are the blues, alright? Now, hidden somewhere out there is a bag of gold. The objective of the game is to locate the bag of gold and get it to the bank. The first team to get the bag of gold into the safe within the bank will be the winners. Now, obviously, pelting the shit out of the opposite team and avoiding being shot yourself is pretty key to all this.'

A single, audible gulp comes from Mother, followed by a second from Duchess. Oh, but they've not heard the worst of it yet...

'You ladies will be playing a stag party today,' he adds.

'You must be joking! We'll be annihilated!' Duchess cries out in disgust.

'Lambs to the slaughter!' Mother wails.

'Not necessarily. We see a lot of male and female teams playing each other. The males often come off worse!' Steve replies, possibly exaggerating the truth a little.

'But surely it's going to hurt!' Duchess contests, hands on hips and wide-eyed.

'Oh, come off it! You've given birth woman. You're a machine! What's a few teeny paintballs in comparison?' Brooke counters.

Duchess goes to speak, then falls silent, outsmarted by Brooke's logic.

'One key thing I'd like you all to remember in the interest of health and safety is not to remove your mask at any point during the game, because a paintball in the eye really *would* bloody hurt, not to mention possibly blind you,' Steve adds, sternly. 'Now, are there any questions?'

Mother and Duchess's hands shoot straight up.

'Yes,' he sighs discreetly in Mother's direction.

'I don't get it,' she squeaks.

He frowns slightly. 'What exactly don't you get?'

'Well, all of it. The entire concept.'

'Ditto!' Duchess agrees stroppily.

'Just get out there, look for the bag of gold, shoot the crap out of your opponents and try not to get shot yourselves in the process. It's really that simple!' he replies. 'Use whatever means available for you to stay undercover. You've got trees, barrels and all sorts out there at your disposal.'

'And how do we shoot the gun?' Mother demands, holding hers up toward him at point blank range.

'Put the gun down!' he booms, moving swiftly to grab the barrel and point it toward the ground. 'Never, ever point the gun off the playing arena when masks aren't being worn!'

'Oh.' Mother pouts, shuffling her feet. 'But you still haven't answered my question, how do you shoot the damn thing?'

'You point it at your target and pull the trigger,' Steve murmurs in disbelief, giving a slight shake of the head.

It's all I can do to contain my laughter as I observe Mother's beady eyes darting this way and that behind her mask, clad in combat gear with her nails painted a shade of frosted heather, clutching her gun. If only those at the infamous country club could see her now!

As we make our way over toward the battlefield, I spy our opponents. Damn. I had hoped for a bunch of weeds not long out of sixth form, but unfortunately they more resemble a load of Navy Seals. And they're laughing at us already. Bastards! In an all-time first, I fear Duchess may be right and annihilation is imminent. Um ... actually, no! The only difference between them and us is that they were born with an ugly-looking set of instruments dangling between their legs and that doesn't make them any better at finding bags of gold, pulling triggers *or* dodging paintballs than we are. I mean, how hard can it be? All we have to do is shoot the gits and find the loot!

Easier said than done I discover soon after the claxon sounds when the battleground instantly becomes a sea of paintballs hurtling through the air. Fuck. Ouch! I've been hit already. How did the fuckers get behind us so quickly? I turn in haste to find Mother standing stationary behind me, aimlessly firing her gun at my arse.

'Stop bloody shooting me, Mother. I'm on your team!' I roar over my shoulder, making a hasty dash to take cover behind the trunk of a large oak to my left.

A loud Liverpudlian catches my attention as he hurls insults our way, laughing his head off as he brutally takes aim at whom, from her tiny frame, I guess is Laura.

Right, he's gonna get it! I move to the next tree to get a closer aim at the pillock, squatting low and pointing the barrel of my gun in his direction. That's it, just a little closer ... BINGO! How do you like that you big walrus?! I find myself giggling like a child as I shoot the crap out of him from behind the safety of my tree, putting an instant end to his jeering as he rubs at his arse, looking around in bewilderment while Laura runs for cover.

Jesus, Brooke is pretty much covered from head to foot already! But she's giving them some back at least, unlike Duchess who I spy crouching behind a barrel with her head down, staying well out of it. Somehow, I resist the temptation to fire at her. Mother is still standing gormlessly in the middle of the battlefield being pelted to shit. Well, at least she's sort of participating, unlike some.

Damn! The walrus has spotted me. I lean back against the tree, observing a plethora of paintballs careering past me and splattering the neighbouring trees. Then nothing. Good! Someone must be giving the brute a taste of his own medicine. Tentatively, I lean out from behind the tree and cop a paintball right on the thigh. Ouch, fuck! He's mere feet away from me now. Right, there's nothing for it, I'm going to have to face the enemy head on.

Like a pound shop GI Jane, I dart out from

behind my tree, making a series of loud sort of Red Indian calls. I don't know why ... An attempt to startle him, possibly? I soon conclude it ineffective as he proceeds to pelt the crap out of me, taking me from Red Indian to Michael Jackson with all the high-pitched 'Oows' that follow. I fire my gun back in his direction, surprised when he drops to his knees howling and clutching his balls. Shit! I may very well have just stopped the walrus from having children ... assuming he hasn't yet sown his horrid seed, that is.

Feeling terrible, I hurry over toward him. 'I'm so sorry, I really didn't mean to go for your family jewels,' I tell him, putting an arm around his shoulders.

'Stupid cow!' he roars up at me, shaking my arm off of him. 'Typical woman resorting to dirty tactics! Well how about I shoot you in the tits? You wouldn't like that, would you?'

'I just told you, I didn't mean to get your gonads. It was a mistake!' I yell back at him. 'Besides, shouldn't you be wearing one of those bollock shields or something?' I challenge.

'We would've done if we were playing blokes,' he groans.

'Well, perhaps that'll teach you not to assume an easy victory just because you're playing against what you clearly see as the weaker sex,' I chastise him.

'Fuck off,' he winces back at me.

I conclude the walrus's pride is probably more dented than his balls as I rush off to alert the marshal.

Marshal alerted, I soon find myself getting shot to shit as I stand scouring the place for any sign of a bag of gold. With my wealth of experience losing car keys and bank cards – which later turn up in ridiculous places – you'd think I'd be good at this, but where the fuck to start? I figure running for cover would be a good first step.

Standing concealed behind a tree, I delight in shooting Monica's opponent while his back is turned. Woo-hoo! This is more fun than I thought. Hey, maybe I should join the army? Nah, let's be real, they'd only let me go within the hour for being a useless twat.

Suddenly, I spy the walrus being helped to his feet by the marshal. Hopefully he'll fuck off out of it now and then … Wait, what?! The bastard's only heading straight back onto the battlefield, playing even more aggressively than before and no doubt seeking vengeance. Bugger. I spot him scanning the trees, clearly looking for me. Considering I'm the chunkiest of our team, it won't be long before he spots me in this hideously oversized combat gear which gives me a shape of a damn Tellytubby. Suddenly, anxiety turns to rage as I watch him swaggering around, giving it the big'un. Horrible sod!

Weaving in and out of the trees, I get into position and begin firing at him from behind.

'Come on then!' he roars, his arms outstretched as he turns in my direction. 'Too chicken, are yer?' he heckles.

That's done it!

Without thinking, I leap out from behind my tree, triggering an almighty shoot-out between the pair of us. The devious git really *is* going for my tits, I think to myself, noting the many paintballs launching straight toward my chest.

'Who's playing dirty now, then?' I screech, dodging out of his target range like a cat on hot bricks, firing my gun non-stop at him. I edge backward, observing him ploughing closer and closer toward me. Oh fuck. Looks like he's trying to get me at point blank range, the bastard! Just as I contemplate going for his balls deliberately this time, the claxon sounds.

'Cease fire! Red team wins!' the marshal shouts.

I glance over toward the bank hut to see an as yet unidentified comrade punching the air victoriously. No way! We won?!

'Fix!' the walrus roars, trudging grumpily over toward his teammates.

Ha! The perfect medicine for his massive ego.

My mouth falls open in shock as our victorious teammate starts belting out a shrilly inapt rendition of "Rule Britannia". What?! It's only bloody Mother! What the actual fuck?!

'You?!' I bellow over toward her in shock.

She nods frantically and does a little jig.

'*You* found the gold?'

'Yes, dear. It's like I've always said to your father, you'll not get anything past me when it comes to money!'

*****

Back at the hotel, Mother announces over afternoon tea that she 'could do with a hair of the dawg'.

'Are you sure that's a good idea?' I ask, feeling slightly strange at being the one cautioning her against drinking when it's always been the other way around.

'This ghastly hangover just won't shift!' she complains, kneading her temples. 'A little hair of the dawg won't do me any harm,' she insists, clicking her fingers at the waitress and ordering a bottle of red. 'Besides, I think my little victory deserves a toast,' she adds, smugly. 'Won't any of you ladies join me for one?'

'Bit early for me,' says Brooke.

'Yeah, same,' Melodie adds.

'Yeah, we really ought to save ourselves for tonight,' Jen chimes in.

What started as a 'hair of the dawg' soon becomes the dog's full bloody coat as a second bottle arrives at the table before too long, with only Mother drinking it.

Oh fuck, the hiccupping's started and she's getting louder and louder by the second, waffling on and on about how Dad killed the new turf in their back garden by over-watering it.

'He never listens, you know … *hic*! Never listens! And there's nothing worse than a know-it-all!'

'Hmph, I'll say!' Duchess scowls, rolling her eyes at us across the table.

'Mother, I really think you should stop at this glass,' I warn, peering around the room in embarrassment. 'How about some lovely refreshing mineral water?' I suggest, gesturing toward the posh bottles on the table.

'Oh, now you sound just like your father. He's a killjoy as well!'

'I'm not being a killjoy, Mother, I'm just worried you're going to embarrass yourself again,' I tell her in a hushed tone through clenched teeth, visions of last night's antics pulsing through my mind.

'No, dear … *hic*! It's you who does that,' she

chortles, taking a dangerously long sip of the umpteenth glass as I close my eyes in dread.

'You know, I'm beginning to see that it's true what they say about money not buying class,' the up until now near-mute Duchess mutters bitchily, spreading a scone thickly with jam and giving Mother daggers across the table.

Bloody hell, here we go.

'Pardon me?' Mother frowns back at her, struggling to focus her eyes.

'Well, my Brian has very generously put you all up in the most expensive hotel in all of London and look at you,' she scoffs, looking down her nose.

'Well, look at *you*! Sat there like mutton … *hic*! … dressed as lamb!' Mother retaliates.

'I beg your pardon?' Duchess fires back at her, enraged.

'Well, your son might call you Duchess, but you're certainly not that! And don't you talk to me about class … *hic!* Us British lead the way where class is concerned, my dear. You Yanks have a lot to learn!'

'Well, at least us Yanks can behave in a dignified manner!' Duchess growls, the over-narrowing of her eyes compensating for her lack of ability to frown.

'Pah! Dignified? You call sitting about with a

face that would turn a funeral up an alley dignified?!'

Duchess's mouth falls open in outrage.

Oh, God. How embarrassing! But still ... *go* Mother!

'Guys, guys! Pack it in now. You're ruining Lizzie's weekend' Brooke quickly interjects as heads begin to turn.

'Pfft! *I'm* doing nothing of the sort. She has her mother to thank for that!' Duchess sneers.

'Do you know, she's going the right way about wearing that ruddy scone?!' Mother barks, slamming her wine glass on the table.

I spy two police officers walking into the dining room. Thankfully they're not here for the gruesome twosome as I soon establish from catching the tail end of mutterings at the table behind about valuables going missing from safes in some of the guest rooms.

They begin making their way around the tables speaking briefly to the guests. It's not long before they arrive at ours.

'Good afternoon, ladies,' officer one greets us on approach.

Mother spins around in her chair, her face suddenly lighting up.

'Goodness, not another lot!' she says, beaming

in delight.

'Sorry?' he remarks.

'Well, we had all this last night! Young Italian lad he was … *hic!* …exceptionally well-endowed!'

The officers look at one another in turn, both wearing puzzled expressions.

'Come on then, let's see what you've got!' she barks, clapping her hands together.

'Madam, we…'

'Mother, stop!' I gasp as she springs up out of her chair, yanks down the zip on officer two's stab vest and attempts to tear the shirt off his back.

'Madam, stop! Stop!' he orders, grappling to bat her away as the entire dining room looks on.

'Give over with your no touching rules!' she trills, scuffling with him to undo the belt on his trousers.

'Madam, this is assault!' officer one booms in disbelief.

'Oh, don't talk wet!' she booms back. 'Come on, off with those trousers!'

Without another word, officer one takes out a pair of handcuffs and forcibly grabs and cuffs Mother while the rest of us look on in horror – all bar Duchess, whom, in an all-time first, is grinning from ear to ear.

'Madam, I'm arresting you for assaulting a police officer. You do not have to say anything, but it may harm your defence if you do not mention when questioned something which you later rely on in court. Anything you do say may be given in evidence. Do you understand?'

'Oooh, would you like me to come quietly officer?' Mother slurs in response, to which he does not appear amused.

'Where are you taking her?' I ask, wide-eyed, still shellshocked at how quickly we went from afternoon tea to Mother's actual arrest.

'West End Central,' officer one replies sternly, marching Mother out of the dining room to the gasps of onlookers.

'Now, I *am* partial to a little brute force, but be gentle with me boys, I'm chair of the women's crochet club on Shaftesbury Avenue, you know, *hic!*' comes the echo of Mother's voice from out in the corridor as she's led away.

Jesus, she *still* thinks they're strippers!

'Ah, hello Lilibeth! How's the weekend going?' Dad chirps, picking up my call moments later.

'Er, well ...'

'How's your mother? Not being too much of a stick-in-the-mud I hope!'

'Actually, she's been arrested, Dad,' I announce, shocked myself at hearing those most unlikely words spoken out loud.

'Arrested?!' he almost chokes back in disbelief.

'Yeah, I'm afraid so. She's been taken to West End Central Police Station.'

'Good grief, whatever for?!'

'For assaulting a police officer,' I reveal, trying to keep my voice down in the busy hotel lobby as though every soul in here hasn't already witnessed Mother being led out in cuffs.

'Is this some sort of wind up?' he half chuckles.

I only wish it bloody was!

'No, it really isn't, Dad. She'd had one too many at afternoon tea and when the Old Bill turned up to investigate some theft at the hotel and started speaking to us, she assumed they were strippers and ... well, she tried to tear their clothes off.'

Silence.

'Dad? You still there?' I ask.

'Yes, love. Pfft, I might have known booze would be behind all this, she's never once tried to tear *my* clothes off throughout our entire marriage!'

'Too much information, Dad,' I mutter, closing my eyes in exasperation.

'Your mother can't handle the drink,' he continues. 'It's always been the same, right from when we were first courting. What the hell was she playing at, drinking to that extent in the afternoon?!'

'Well, she won at paintballing and she had a hang ... er ... she thought a couple of drinks would help her headache,' I lie.

'Paintballing?! Your mother won at paintballing?! I told her to get involved and enjoy herself for your sake, but Christ, sounds like she's off the bloody wall! And I'll bet she was on the booze last night as well, wasn't she?!' Dad demands.

'Well, she just had a few,' I tell him, deciding not to mention Fabio and his massive knob.

'Right, I'm going to go down there now and find out what the hell's happening,' he announces, swiftly hanging up the phone.

With Mother in the nick, we decide it wouldn't feel right going out partying. The girls take themselves off for some spa treatments while I'm holed up in our room glued to my phone for updates, ordering a shit tonne of room service on Brian's tab while I still have the chance. I'm thoroughly dreading the looming resumption of grapefruits for breakfast.

A text finally pings around 7pm:

They've let her off with a caution. I've taken her

home to spare you both any further embarrassment! Dad x

It later transpires at the airport next morning that Dad's efforts to spare me any further embarrassment were all in vain when my handbag is removed from the conveyer belt and opened for inspection by security who have to remove around fifty Celebrations sweet wrappers in full view of onlookers before they can get to its actual contents!

Chapter 11:

Back to reality

They say absence makes the heart grow fonder, don't they? Just not in my case, it would seem.

I had quietly assumed I would return back from London and my relationship with Brian would've resolved itself as if by magic, that long absent spark re-igniting all by itself. But no such luck. Everything is just as it was: the brief pecks, the watching me like a hawk where food is concerned, the frostiness, the alarming lack of sex – I can't actually remember the last time Brian and I slept together.

With my hen weekend now a distant memory, no improvement in things with Brian, and a little over a fortnight to go until the wedding, I feel more trapped and desperate than ever, particularly upon taking delivery of – and trying on – my custom-made French designer wedding dress which, *quelle surprise*, is tighter than a hangman's fucking knot! What the hell? Have I seriously put on *that* much weight since Paris, or has Pierre Dupont pissed up the measurements? I tell myself it's the latter, but as I wriggle myself out of the tourniquet gown, the sight of everything wobbling in the mirror would suggest otherwise! Still happier blaming Pierre Dupont, though.

'Oh fuck. Oh fuck!' I wail, going all hot as it dawns on me that it would take a sodding miracle for it to fit in time for the big day. Shit! Brian will hit the roof when he finds out. My changing proportions have already cost him a fortune. There's got to be something I can do, anything!

'Shall I send you my girdle by airmail?' Mother suggests during my frantic phone call to her.

Er, just not *that!*

'I think it's a bit beyond girdles!' I pant down the line. 'What I want to know is, is there anything a seamstress can do? Oh, please tell me there is, please!'

She clicks her tongue. 'Well, they can let it out dear, but not by *three* dress sizes.'

'Three?!' I splutter, repulsed. 'I know I've put on weight, but I'm still way smaller than I was. What about all that weight I lost?'

'Well, you've found it again, dear.'

Wow.

*****

'Hmm, it's certainly on the snug side!' the seamstress remarks carefully when I pull back the musty cubicle curtain of her downtown shop late that afternoon to reveal my caterpillar-like silhouette strangled within the Pierre Dupont creation.

'Is there anything you can do? Anything at all?' I ask in desperation.

'Well, if it were a zipper fastening I could have converted it to a corset back and it would've been problem solved,' she muses, looking me up and down. 'Of course, the problem we have is that it's already a corset back.'

No shit.

'So, are you saying it's not possible to let out a corset back dress?' I ask, catching sight of myself in the full-length mirror opposite and shamefacedly averting my eyes.

'I have a one-inch window either side of the dress to play with, that's about it,' she reveals.

'Well, how big a window would it take for this thing to fit?'

'As it stands right now, probably three to four inches,' she guesses, her tone laced with doubt.

Hm, not too bad. I was actually expecting double figures.

'I'll lose weight!' I say, as though it's piss-easy. 'I can lose two inches before the wedding.'

'Hm, that could work. How long do you have?' she asks.

'Two weeks,' I reply, observing her mouth falling open and her glasses all but steaming up in shock.

I leave $150 lighter but with the weight of the world on my shoulders vis-à-vis how I'm going to lose two actual inches off my waist in an effing fortnight!

Me: *Food is not a hobby, it's fuel. Food is not a hobby, it's fuel. Food is not a hobby, it's fuel.*

Also me: *Food is life!*

Well, it is, isn't it? Calories are in everything we do, lurking around every sodding corner!

'Oh, what a lovely day! Shall we have a BBQ?' CALORIES!

'Look how sunny it is out, shall we go for a picnic?' CALORIES!

'Fancy going to the cinema?' CALORIES!

'Shall we watch a movie tonight?' CALORIES!

Shall we go to the pub?' EMPTY FUCKING CALORIES!

Back in the car, I whip out my phone to consult the ingenious all-knowing Google.

"How to rapidly lose inches …"

"Body wrap." Cue horrific memories of answering the door to my landlord semi-naked in an algae body wrap.

"Cabbage soup diet." Fuck that!

"Limit carb intake." Ugh!

"Limit sugar intake." Ughhh!

"Get a waist trainer."

*****

'Why are you walking like a dick?' Brooke quizzes, looking up from her desk as I arrive at work next morning in the manner of someone stuck in a straitjacket.

'Waist trainer. Evil, evil waist trainer,' I reply her breathlessly.

She pulls a face. 'Pfft! Too little too late, chick!'

'Well, desperate times call for desperate measures,' I grimace in my defence. 'Anyway, if it's good enough for the Kardashians—'

'Then you know it's a shit idea!' she interjects.

'Well, I'm willing to try anything. The wedding's now less than a fortnight away!' I remind her, taking out my meal replacement shake from my bag and placing it by my desk.

'Good luck with *that!*' she scoffs, rolling her eyes.

'Look, I've got to try something. You're supposed to be my friend, you should be cheering me on!' I huff, struggling to sit down.

'That's exactly why I'm *not* cheering you on, Lizzie. This is all wrong! It comes to something when it's easier to sit starving in a vice all day than go to the man who should be your biggest supporter in life,' she counters. 'Your problems are Brian's problems too. It's pretty crap that you can't go to him about something as small as a dress not fitting.'

'Er, hello?' I splutter. 'We aren't just talking high street frocks here. We're talking about a wedding gown worth thousands of dollars,' I point out, 'and it's the second one he's paid for already. I'm going to be able to open my own sodding bridal shop at the rate I'm going. I've cost him an arm and a leg, Brooke, he'll go batshit!'

'The guy's a billionaire, Lizzie. Nothing costs an arm and a leg when you've more dough than you know what to do with. It's nothing to him and if he really loves you, he wouldn't go batshit about it. He should value *you* over money,' she reasons. 'Besides, it was him who insisted on you having only the best, anyway. You could've easily bought something from a high street salon yourself, but he wanted to go all-out. I mean, yeah, it's a waste, but you can always sell the dresses on. You're a wedding planner, you speak to brides every day. It's really not the end of the world.'

I pause momentarily in defeat before springing up out of my chair, hoisting up my blouse, tearing off the waist trainer and chucking it across the room in disgust. And, breathe! Bugger me, where do those Kardashians get off, squashing their entrails?!

'So, what are you going to do?' Brooke badgers, as if I might have some clue.

Sinking into my chair, I burst into tears.

'It's all such a m-mess,' I sob into my hands.

'You really need to talk to Brian,' she soothes, draping an arm around my shoulder.

'But things are so s-shit between us. He's h-hardly around and when he is, his head's stuck in a sodding newspaper,' I wail.

'Well, things can't go on like this, you're about to marry the guy! Look, it's Saturday. It's quiet. You should go home, fix you both some drinks and get things out in the open. Find out what's on his mind. Have a heart to heart, you know?'

She's right, although it's been dressed up to sound a lot simpler than it is. How on earth am I to even broach the subject?

'Oh yeah, Brian? You know all that dough you paid Pierre Dupont for my wedding dress? Well, you might as well have wiped your arse on it because there's more chance you being blown by the Pope than it fitting me.'

'P.S. I heart food!'

I spend the car journey home psyching myself up for that heart to heart. You never know, he could be really nice about things. Maybe I've been blowing everything up in my mind to be way bigger than it actually is. Second-guessing has always been my problem. Perhaps he's just stressed with work? Maybe it's pre-wedding nerves? Brooke's right, it's the weekend! Let's just chill with drinks, have a bit of lunch and talk it over.

Or not, as I soon determine when he arrives home early from golf and catches me unawares at the fridge – totally not how it was supposed to go and shit for two reasons:

1. He can now observe for himself precisely why my wedding dress doesn't fit.
2. All that talk of a healthy balanced conception diet!

'You're home early,' he remarks, frostily.

So is he, dammit!

'What are you doing?!' he snorts, arriving at the fridge wide-eyed and appalled.

'I was … just getting a drink,' I say.

'You drink condensed milk straight outta the can?' he challenges with furrowed brows.

'Um, sometimes.'

He pulls a contemptuous expression.

'You don't?' I ask, instantly regretting putting such a question to a man who only eats in the finest Michelin three-star restaurants.

The look he gives me serves as an emphatic 'no'.

'Okay, two things,' he begins in his scary CEO voice. 'First, you're eating crap again after everything we discussed about conceiving another child ...'

'It's only condensed milk!' I shrug in my defence.

'Lizzie, get outta town! You think I'm an idiot?' he rages. 'Mom told me what you ate in London *and* about all those fucking candy wrappers at airport security. Plus, I have your room service bill! I guess this is where you tell me it was all your girlfriends and you were living off of air the whole time, right?'

Looking shadily from side to side, I'm rendered momentarily speechless as visions of Duchess eagerly reporting back every calorie consumed play out in my mind. Kill! Kill! Kill!

'And *second*,' he goes on, waving my box of contraceptive pills in my face, 'I found these out on the side in the en suite bathroom.'

Bollocks! I must've forgotten to put them back after I took one this morning.

'So, what is it? You don't want to have kids? Is

that what this is?!' he demands.

At first - and as with any line of questioning from since the age of about six whether innocent or not – my go-to reaction would be "deny, deny, deny". But as I stand squirming in the toe-curling silence that follows, I conclude now might be time for the truth. Finally.

'Speak to me!' he booms, making me feel as though I'm back in the principal's office.

'You're r-right, I don't want kids,' I eventually stammer, falling short of saying not now and possibly not ever with *him*.

He stares at me speechless as I try to find the words to give him some kind of an explanation.

'Things … Things aren't good between us, Brian. You must've noticed?'

He looks at me blankly for a moment. 'Things were great 'til you changed!' he accuses.

Oh. How didn't I guess this was all *my* fault?

'I changed? How?!' I challenge, open-mouthed.

'Gee, where do I start!' he exclaims. 'You're undisciplined. Unmotivated. It's like you've morphed into this person I barely recognise. You've totally given up and let yourself go. What happened to the woman I fell in love with? What is it, grief? Is it grief? I mean, what's happened to you!?'

'Nothing's happened to me, Brian, I'm the same bloody person!' I fire back at him.

'Well, if that were the case, there wouldn't be an issue,' he mumbles, looking me up and down suggestively.

'Excuse me?!' I gasp, seeing red. 'Yeah, I'm eating shit. Yeah, I've gained weight, but this is me! What's the matter, am I not good enough for you anymore?!'

The silence that follows does all the talking.

'Your words, not mine,' he manages, eventually.

'Come off it, it's obvious that's what you're alluding to. It's written all over your face!' I half yell, my voice ducking briefly as I picture the butler outside the door with a pad and pen, taking notes.

'Don't be stupid,' he mutters, not even trying to sound convincing. 'I just want to … I just want to get back to how it was at the beginning.'

'And I suppose if I were to just shrink back to a size eight everything would be hunky-dory, right?' I guess.

He says nothing.

'Don't you put all of this on me, Brian! Don't you dare!' I rage. 'I've been going stir-crazy, beating my brain out trying to get just an ounce of your attention!'

He looks at me as if I should already know I'm not doing it for him anymore. 'I don't have the highest sex drive Lizzie but … well, it's like you don't even try anymore. You never wear any of that nice underwear I bought you,' he complains.

I would if I could fit my arse into it!

'You've resigned yourself to wearing those God-awful passion killer panties,' he goes on, making me turn red in the face. 'And this, this doesn't help anything,' he declares, picking up and slamming down that sinful tin of milk on the counter in disgust.

Mental note: *Totally not the time to mention that wedding dress number two doesn't fit!*

'Oh, give over, Brian!' I fume. 'It would be impossible to steal you away from business even if you were a bleeding nympho of the highest order!'

'Well forgive me for trying to earn a fucking living, Lizzie! Gee, I give you everything, everything you could ever want, and it's still not enough?! Boy, I'm beginning to see that Mom was right about you.'

'Meaning?!'

'Well, you want too much. Nothing's ever good enough. You're too demanding!'

Stopping short at slapping him, I launch into a furious tirade. 'I have never once asked you for a thing!' I screech in outrage. 'All I've ever wanted is your time, Brian. You were the one falling over yourself to plough your cash into my business, but I didn't take a dime from you. Not a fucking dime! I earn my own money. All these swanky fucking weekends away, the wedding dress designer, the car you insisted I needed, the meals out, the fucking Rolex – all *your* choice, not mine,' I remind him, taking a deep breath. 'And you know what? All *this*,' I scoff, gesturing toward the finery surrounding us, 'it means shit to me!'

He stares at me for a few moments, perplexed.

'What do you want, Lizzie? What is it you actually want, 'cos I'm damned if I know!'

I stare up at him momentarily, my eyes welling.

'I just want to be *me*, Brian. To be loved for who I am. *Not* for the way I look. *Not* for what I eat. *Not* for my business acumen. For *me*.'

Silence.

'Say something!' I sob, not sure exactly what I want to hear, as he frowns back at me in bewilderment.

'What do you want me to say?' he sighs, breezing out of the kitchen and leaving me staring at the floor in a daze, my suspicions more or less confirmed that he was only ever in love with whom he and I both thought I was.

*****

Reeling, my mind turning over endless echoes of Brian's cutting words, I yank out the diamond encrusted stud earrings he bought me for my thirtieth and place them down upon the posh, polished dressing table next to that hideous Rolex. I wiggle off my engagement ring and place it down too, somehow overcoming the urge to throw it.

Pausing thoughtfully, I hoist my work skirt up around my waist and wiggle out of the immense, nude maternity knickers I've thus far been unable to bring myself to bin on account of how insanely comfy they are. But, alas! They originate from a pack of three purchased with Brian's dirty cash and must therefore be outlawed along with anything else he ever bought me. Hmph, I'll show him how accurate Duchess' assumptions are about me – he can even have the cacks off my arse complete with stink of the day, I think to myself, holding them up in all their stupendous glory.

'Farewell. my friends,' I bid them, tossing them into the wash basket and wiggling into one of only a few pairs I can be sure I purchased myself on account of them being faded and knackered-out from all those too hot washes back in the good old days when I did my own laundry.

Safe in the knowledge that every thread I'm

wearing was bought and paid for by my own means, I fish my trusty fake Louis tote out of the wardrobe, which, co-incidentally, I never did get round to unpacking from last time I was leaving. Convenient!

My phone pings with a text confirming my cab's arrival outside.

Time to go ... for *real* this time.

Thinking better of farting on Brian's side of the bed before departing, I give a brief glance around what was almost our marital bedroom on my way out the door, wondering what I would miss about no longer being Brian's little woman – correction, not little *enough* woman. By the time I reach the bottom of the fuck-off grand staircase, I still haven't come up with anything.

Wow, this is it, I think to myself, now resolute in my convictions that Brian and I are done. *Finito*. Kaput. His expressionless face as he strolls into the entrance hall and observes me stood by the door with my bag at my feet all but confirms that notion.

We stare at each other blankly for a few moments and I hesitate, with just the tiniest part of me hoping he'll beg me to stay.

He doesn't.

'I'm leaving, Brian,' I announce, as if he might not know.

He nods, placing both his hands into the pockets of his posh, designer slacks.

'I think it's for the best, don't you?' I add, looking to get some kind of reaction out of him.

Silence.

'Well, aren't you going to say anything?!' I huff, folding my arms.

'Okay,' he shrugs.

'That it?!' I scoff.

'What else is there to say?' he remarks dismissively before his cell starts ringing and he takes it out of his pocket. 'Gus, hey!' he answers in a manner markedly different to one you'd expect from someone whose relationship is ending before their eyes.

Wow.

To think of the time I wasted fretting about leaving him heartbroken and it turns out he couldn't give two shiny shits.

'Goodbye, Brian!' I snort in dismay, tearing open the front door and slamming it hard behind me as I storm over to my waiting cab.

A showreel of our entire relationship barely flickers in my mind as the wheels of my cab crunch the gravel on exit down the long winding driveway out of Brian's life.

I don't look back. Not once. Well, there's no use

crying over condensed milk, is there?

Chapter 12:

What Now?

'I've done it! I've finally left that stuck-up, business-obsessed, arrogant arsehole!' I announce victoriously down the phone from the back seat of the cab whisking me away to freedom as I speak.

Silence.

'Hello?' I enquire.

'Wow. Didn't realise you felt that strongly!' comes Brian's voice at the other end.

I go all stiff, dropping my phone in the footwell in the scrabble to hang up quick enough. Fuck! I must've called Brian instead of Brooke. Damn their close association in my contacts list! Damn! Damn! Damn!

I observe the cab driver's beady eyes studying me curiously through the rear-view mirror.

'Don't you just hate technology?' I fake laugh, cringing and flushing pink as I fish for my phone.

'Yah, never been one for gadgets,' he agrees.

A brief silence ensues.

'Er ... I don't mean to pry and all, but he must be a total schmuck for you to walk out and leave all *that* behind,' he remarks dangerously. 'I mean the size of that place back there, woo!' He gives a slight whistle as I sink back into my seat, partly shocked at his forwardness but simultaneously at ease with his calming voice and cuddly John Candy-esque exterior. Suddenly, I look at this total stranger as my very own Uncle Buck and it all comes tumbling out.

'Well, yes. He *is* a total schmuck,' I agree steadfastly. 'We were supposed to get married in a fortnight, would you believe?!'

'Holy smokes, did he cheat on you?' my sudden, unlikely therapist enquires.

'Only with the *Financial Times*,' I huff, 'but he did put me on a diet.'

'He did that?!'

'Yes, *and* he was always catching me at the fridge!'

'Jeez!'

'*And* he's a Mummy's boy!'

'Oof!'

'*And* he didn't like my wind!'

A silence follows before all four of the electric windows suddenly begin opening partially. Cab

Man thinks I'm a fart bag!

'And, to be perfectly honest, he's an insufferably boring, pyjama-folding nincompoop and the sex was crap!' I declare unapologetically, rounding up my one-star review of Brian Garcia. Well, almost. 'Oh, yes, and he wears the most dreadful fucking slippers ever!' I add to the tirade.

'Did the guy have *any* good qualities?' Cab Man asks.

I suck in my teeth, my mind turning over almost two years of Brian-data in search of any.

'Well, he makes a very nice cappuccino,' I manage.

'That it?'

'Pretty much,' I conclude.

'Whatever attracted you to him in the first place, then?' he asks.

'Not his millions, if that's what you're thinking!' I exclaim over-defensively. 'And it's a long story, but in a nutshell, I had come out of another relationship back in the UK – the love of my bloody life, actually, but that's another story – and, well, it had been a while since I'd had any male attention, so when I moved here and started at my new job, I met Brian, he asked me out to dinner and it felt right, you know?'

He nods, leaning across and opening the glove

box, taking out a large bag of opened popcorn.

'Go on,' he prompts, devouring a fistful and listening intently.

'Well, he was my boss, so I was a little cautious at first, but he seemed so lovely. He was really good to me at the beginning when I was a size eight, treated me like a princess,' I reveal thoughtfully. 'Then I got pregnant and he was over the moon, but I lost the baby and it basically all went tits-up after that. I put weight on and he got cold. He made himself totally unavailable to me. Was always busy with work. His phone never stopped ringing, head always in a newspaper,' I trawl, vaguely aware of car horns sounding as the cab drifts over into the next lane of traffic with the cabbie now fully engrossed and otherwise engaged in the gory details of my tumultuous love split.

'SHIT!' He gulps, placing both hands on the wheel and steering back into his lane. He sighs in relief. 'Listen, a guy who can't handle you at your worst sure doesn't deserve you at your best,' he remarks sincerely.

'I know, right? Anyway, we stopped sleeping together weeks ago,' I continue, still not quite believing I'm having this conversation. 'I tried so hard to make it work but, well, I've never really gotten over my ex, truth be told. Dan was so ... he was so genuine. I wasn't always a size eight you know. I was a twenty-two when Dan and I were an item, but he loved me for *me*. Just the way I was,' I muse dreamily.

'Then why the hell d'ya leave the guy?' he splutters in disbelief, spraying the dash with bits of popcorn.

'Er, I didn't think it was authentic,' I tell him, making the probably wise split-second decision not to mention that ridiculous love spell!

'How come?' he quizzes.

'I guess it all felt too good to be true, someone so dreamy loving *me*,' I reason.

'So, what changed?'

'Well, Brian and I took a trip back to the UK last December to spend Christmas with my parents,' I explain. 'I bumped into Dan at the airport and he told me he still loves me and always did. Then he came to my folks' place and proposed to me w- with his Nan's ring,' I sniff, voice breaking.

'And?'

'Well, I told him I'd think about it, but then I found out I was pregnant to Brian and I had to turn him down.'

'Even though you were certain this Dan guy was, and still is, the one?' Cab Man enquires.

'God, yeah. Even when things were great with Brian, there was always something off. Some-

A KIND OF TRAGIC WEDDING

thing missing. It was like, you know when you paint your fingernails yourself?'

'Er, no. But go on.'

'Well, you always paint one hand perfectly with your dominant hand and the second hand always turns out that bit crapper. It's like, even with everything Brian had and the kind of life he could give me, Dan was always the perfect hand and Brian the not-so-perfect one.'

Cab Man lets out a deep exhalation of breath. 'You want me to take you straight to JFK? Sounds like you need to get your ass on a plane and go find this fella before it's too late,' he suggests urgently.

'No, no!' I laugh, dismissively. 'It's been months. Dan will have long moved on by now.'

Although I sincerely fucking hope he hasn't!

'In my experience, when a guy's in that deep, he never truly moves on,' he reveals, hinting at his own heartache.

In stark contrast to him, I decide not to pry. Besides, we're only a street away from work now, there's no time for any further heart-rendering break-up tales. Mine's has taken up the whole effing journey I'm not about to sit with the meter running while he tells me *his!*

'Anyway,' I muse thoughtfully, 'I'm barely out of Brian's door. There's still stuff to go over with him before I even think about getting into another relationship,' I tell both Cab Man and myself.

'Tomorrow isn't promised to any of us,' he cautions, giving me a knowing look through the rear-view mirror.

'Well, thank you. You're a really good listener,' I praise, bringing the conversation to a swift close and climbing out as we draw up outside work.

'Anytime,' he chuckles.

Crouching beside his door, I rifle through my purse.

'Hey, I think you did the right thing and I think you know that too.' He winks up at me.

I give a nod and a meek smile.

'When something feels right, it gets you right here, *right* in your gut,' he chirps, thumping the Mr Greedy belly straining beneath his shirt.

I find myself suddenly feeling sorry for him for no reason, sat behind the wheel all jolly and rosy-cheeked but possibly unlucky in love. Ugh. Why do I do this?! *Why* do I always feel sorry for nice people for no reason whatsoever? The thought of him driving off alone, disappearing into the abyss is so sad – even though it's generally what happens when one disembarks a cab. It's his bloody job for effs sake! And there's nothing to suggest any harm or misfortune will come to him. *God*, I'm a knob.

'Listen, if you change your mind and you need a ride to the airport, give me a shout,' he says, handing me his business card.

'Thanks.' I smile, feeling suddenly better now that I have the means to call this total stranger should I wish to ever check that he hasn't been mugged or made homeless and that somebody loves him. 'Keep the change,' I tell him, thrusting a $100 bill his way.

Mental note: *Must reign in massive tips now am no longer betrothed to filthy-rich but boring billionaire.*

'Heart to heart went well then?' Brooke remarks, looking up from her desk as I trundle in through the front door, dropping the Louis tote heavily at my feet.

'Even better than I thought' I reflect coolly. 'I've left him, he couldn't give a fuck and it looks like the wedding's off.'

'YASSSSSS! Put it right there, girlfriend!' she sings, leaping out of her desk chair and rushing over to high five me. 'Any regrets?'

'None what-so-fucking-ever!' I declare unwaveringly.

*****

'Wow. This place doesn't get any cleaner!' I remark, breezing in through the door to Brooke's apartment and collapsing on the sofa in a weary heap.

Feeling something digging into my side, I pull out an empty plastic bottle buried down the side of the seat pad. 'Shit, is this my age-old protein shake from way back when?'

'No,' she says defensively. 'Well … I dunno, it could be.'

'Ewww, Brooke! That was *ages* ago when I put looks before food!'

'So? I've been busy, haven't I?'

'I don't know, have you?'

She falls suspiciously silent before saying, 'Look, I've been meaning to tell you, but I didn't think I should just yet. You know, because of everything going on with you and Brian.'

'What is it?' I frown up at her, wondering what on earth could be coming next.

'I've been seeing this guy…'

'Not Daisy-man?!' I gasp in horror.

'No, no. He's called Tom,' she reveals. 'How cool is the association with Tom Hardy though?!'

'He looks like Tom Hardy?'

'No, I mean that he's called Tom, like Tom Hardy, yeah? Anyway, things are getting serious,' she says with a half smirk.

'As in "he's a sadist" serious or "falling in love" serious?'

She smiles dreamily. 'Falling in love serious.'

Phew!

'Oh,' I exclaim in surprise. 'Oh, right.'

'Aren't you happy for me?' she asks, biting her lip apprehensively.

'Of course, I'm happy for you!' I insist. 'It's just that it's come as a total surprise. I didn't even have an inkling. You didn't let on whatsoever!'

'Well, you were having a tough time and I didn't want to rub your face in it.'

'Look, you're my best mate. You wouldn't have been rubbing my face in it. Your happiness is *my* happiness, right?' I assure her with my sweetest BFF smile.

'Right!' She grins. 'Oh, I'm so glad it's all out in the open. Now I can tell you all about his massive dong!'

'Oh, rub my face in it, why don't you?!' I scoff, sweet BFF smile dropping somewhat.

'Oh my God, it's been amazing, Lizzie. He's so amazing! He knows I'm a virgin and he said it was a rare and wonderful thing. He wants to wait and make my first time super special. How sweet is that? I mean, we've done pretty much everything else you can do in the sack and I've told him I'm perfectly ready to ride him, but he still thinks we should wait. Aw, he's so wonderful, I so can't wait for you to meet him!'

'Great. That's really great!' I enthuse, suddenly feeling very single and sex-starved.

'Look, this is him,' she gushes, holding out her phone upon which I observe a loved-up selfie of the pair of them virtually eating each other alive!

'Well, I can't really see his face,' I point out.

'Ooh, yeah, hang on a sec,' she giggles, swiping furiously through her camera roll. 'Ooh, this is a lush one!' she announces, handing her phone to me at which point I blink and blink again in horror at the image of what I assume is a graphic close up of her perineum ... or Tom's perhaps, who knows?!

'What the fuck's *this*?' I gasp in horror.

'Shit! N-no, that's not him,' she gabbles, snatching the phone back. 'Sorry, must've overswiped. This is him,' she grins, proudly holding up a photo of Tom's actual face.

Hm. He's cute. A little too surfer dude for my liking, but cute.

'He looks nice,' I enthuse. 'Anyway, what *was* that?' I repeat, screwing my face up in disgust with part of me thinking I may be better off not knowing.

'It's nothing,' she dismisses casually, as though everyone has these sorts of photos on their camera rolls. 'I just thought that now I got a fella, I should start waxing down there, you know? And I needed to see if I'd done my ass properly. 'Cos, like, you can never really be sure, can you?'

'Didn't you think to delete it straight after?' I probe, gawking at her in disbelief.

'I was gonna, but then I thought I saw a haemorrhoid, even though I don't really know what they look like, so I thought I should keep it and get a second opinion.'

I stare at her numbly.

'Well?' she asks.

'Well, what?'

'Did you see any haemorrhoids?'

'I don't know, Brooke, I was that traumatised I wasn't really looking for piles!'

'Oh, here you go then,' she says, unashamedly forcing that horrific image on me again for a second time.

'Gah! Take it away! Take it away!' I yell, battling to un-see it. 'I ain't no bleeding health expert, go and see a damn doctor!'

'Hm, maybe I'll just ask Tom to have a look when he's next down there,' she muses.

'If you want to keep this oracle of a bloke of yours, then I really wouldn't,' I caution.

If she's anything like me, she may very well fart on him!

'Why? It's nothing he hasn't seen already,' she dismisses, beaming as a text from The Oracle himself arrives.

'Aww, he misses my face!' she coos.

Hm, not sure how long I'm going to be able to endure the giggly, loved-up Tom-talk!

'Please tell me you and this Tom haven't been at it in here!' I shout from the doorway to my former bedroom door. 'It smells kinda funky!'

'Oh, that'll be Barry!' she shouts back matter-of-factly.

I very nearly choke. 'Barry?! Just how many men have you got on the go?!'

'No, Barry's a turtle! Tom's landlord got all funny with him about keeping Barry at his place, so I said he could keep him here in the spare room. You'll love him, he's super cute!'

Love *that* and its hum? I don't think so! But if she and this Tom do then perhaps they should start their own bizarrely named candle line à la Gwyneth Paltrow – "This Smells Like Barry's Shit", or similar.

'Is there any other species in here, stuffed or alive, you need to tell me about?' I shout back, hurrying to open the window and pausing by Dirty Barry's tank which sits reeking on top of the chest of drawers. I peer through the glass. He stares back at me, anything but cute, his depressingly glum puss instantly reminding me of Duchess!

*****

'So, how do you like Barry?' Brooke beams over Cosmos in Rudey's.

'He smells of arse!' I huff unapologetically.

'Aw, I thought you'd be made up to have a little roommate,' she coos.

'I have enough of those in the bloody wardrobe!' I remind her, trying not to think about her Norman Bates-esque collection of stuffed cats languishing in there.

'Why are you so down in the dumps, Lizzie? You're single now, just like you wanted. No more boring Brian! No more douchebag Duchess! No more food surveillance! Your heart should be overflowing with the joy of living again.'

She's right. It wasn't supposed to be like this. This isn't at all how I'd expected to feel after breaking free from Brian's shackles. Why do I feel like this?!

I say nothing, stabbing at the ice in my Cosmo with a straw.

'Is it because of Tom?' she asks, suddenly.

'No. No, of course not,' I fraudulently reassure.

It's not that I'm not totally psyched she's found happiness. I *am*. It's just Tom's sudden arrival on the scene has sparked a swift and scary transition from "slim and engaged" to "tubby third wheel"! Suddenly, I feel like Cinderella, sat in rags beside her little mice friends at five past midnight when all the magic's run out.

Expectation: *Free, liberated single female high on life.*

Reality: *Sad singleton gooseberry high on turtle toilet!*

Verdict: *Considering calling Brian to suggest second go at relationship if only for cleaner quality of air!*

'Aww, good. Because he's joining us any minute now,' Brooke announces, knocking back her cocktail.

Before I can utter a word, I spy the infamous Tom, identifiable by his wavy dirty blonde surfer dude locks, sneaking up behind Brooke's chair with a finger pressed to the giant grin on his lips.

'BOO!' he yells, causing her to spin around in shock before they both emit a series of high-pitched, sickeningly loved-up squeals and proceed to snog each other's faces off without shame, like they're the only ones in the room.

Christ, are they seriously doing tongues?!

One minute on: Still snogging.

Two minutes on: *Still* snogging!

I hurriedly take out my phone and begin typing a load of guff in the Notes app to give the impression I'm texting someone, when in reality my phone hasn't pinged once all night. Not bloody once! Certainly not from Brian and not even from Mother.

Just as I give serious thought to calling Cab Man for counselling, the lovebirds come up for air.

'Oh, hee hee! Lizzie, this is Tom. Tom, Lizzie,' Brooke finally manages.

Hee hee? Who does she think she is, MJ?!

'Hey there,' he grins. 'Snookums has told me a lot about you, haven't you Snookums?'

'Oh?' I half laugh, sincerely hoping Snookums hasn't said too much.

'Don't worry, all good,' he grins with a pause I don't like. 'Well, except for you thinking Marshall Jefferson was president,' he adds, bursting into hysterics.

My face falls. 'So? I got him mixed up with J.F Kennedy,' I reason, quickly realising how dissimilar the two sound and muttering something about not being good with initials.

Well, Snookums still thinks it's Urethra Franklin, but I stop short of telling him that, deciding it would only make me appear bitchy. He'll find out for himself soon enough, anyway. It's only a matter of time before she assaults his eardrums with that album.

I knock back my cocktail and make a quick dash for the ladies, mumbling to myself along the way, as you do.

'This is ridiculous! Have they *no* thought whatsoever for little old me, fresh out of a break-up while they're sitting about drinking each other up like Pammie Anderson and Tommy Lee? Christ, she was a virgin at thirty, now you'd think she was some sort of sex guru! Hmph, well, I refuse to be the third bloody wheel all night. *Must* think of an excuse to leave. *Must* think of an excuse to leave! Even if I'll only be going back to Dirty Barry!'

I wander out of the cubicle having relieved myself just as the toilet door squeaks open and some bloke walks in.

I freeze.

He freezes.

Suddenly, I conclude Mother's rape alarm was probably a good call. Oh, but it's not in my handbag. In fact, I haven't seen the bloody thing for months. Bugger.

'Don't come any closer!' I yell toward him, not entirely sure what I would do if he did.

He gives me a 'calm your tits' sort of look.

'It's alright, it's okay, I must've taken the wrong door by mistake,' he says, holding his hands up.

'Good, because I'm a black belt in karate, mate!' I tell him in an unconvincing mousey voice, breathing a sigh of relief as he disappears out the door.

Moments later, it squeaks back open. Oh, fuck. He's back, and he's not going to leave until he's had a piece of me! Help!

'*You're* the one who took the wrong damn door!' he snorts, looking pissed off and striding over toward the urinals I had somehow, up to now, failed to notice.

Oh. I'm in the Gents. And he *doesn't* want a piece of me ... much like the rest of the male population, it would seem.

Chapter 13:

Do I, Don't I?

As Sunday morning dawns, I wake to Barry's stench – which I swear I could smell in my sleep – and an empty flat. Oh. Brooke didn't come home last night and is now obviously lying in bed with The Oracle in a delightfully Barry-odour-free zone, somewhere.

I wonder:

A: Should I attempt to clean out Barry's tank before he, I, or both of us, die from the stench?

B: Is it time to call Brian to finalise our split?

Option B is taken out of my hands when *he* calls me, and I decide against A, having concluded that I'm already going through enough shit without adding Barry's to it.

'Heavy night last night?' Brian remarks, without so much as a 'hello'.

'No, why?'

'I got a text alert saying you'd arrived at some trashy downtown bar.'

Shit! Must delete that app the second I am off the phone!

'And what of it?!' I fire up. 'It's not really your business what I do anymore, is it?'

'Fair enough,' he mutters. 'I was just calling to ask for a forwarding address to send your stuff on to.'

'I took everything I needed,' I reply, cold as ice.

He sighs. 'You sure? There's a tonne of handbags and clothes. Guess I should donate them all to goodwill, then.'

'Good idea! You do that, Brian,' I agree.

Ha! No amount of reverse psychology's gonna work on me, mate.

'Fine. Mom's been taking care of cancelling all aspects of the wedding, so you don't have to concern yourself with any of that.'

Bugger me, *she* doesn't piss about, does she?!

'Good!' I reply.

'Okay then.'

'Okay then!'

Beep beep beep

He's gone.

So, that's it! All ties cut with Brian Garcia.

I languish on the sofa, lost in reflection. So, what now? What's next for Lizzie Bradshaw?

Voice in head: *Dan! Dan! Dan! Dan! Dan! Dan! Dan! Dan! Dan! Dan! Dan! Dan! Dan! Dan! Dan! Dan!*

Throughout all of this, the tide of feelings I have for him has never gone out. It's always remained, lapping steadfast upon the sands of time. Even so, I can't just expect him to be single. He's more than likely moved on. After all, he's spent all this time thinking I'm heavily pregnant and soon to be wed with zero possibility of any second chance for us. Still, I suppose there's nothing wrong with calling him as a friend. Just because you call someone, it doesn't necessarily mean you want to shag the arse off them, does it? Well, it does in my case, but just saying…

You know what? Sod it! I'm gonna call him … Ah, no I'm not! The other SIM card with his phone number is in that Kate Spade bag, the one Brian's about to give to goodwill. Oh, fuck! Dan's number shall be destined for the abyss, hidden in the depths of a handbag that's going to wind up smelling like a stale digestive biscuit in some thrift shop!

Right, there's only one point of contact left to try. Facebook. Thank God for the Zuckerberg!

Tongue out, I load the app and launch my first guilt-free search for Mr Wonderful. Frowning, I scroll through the results. There is umpteen Dan Elliotts, but none of them Mr Wonderful. *What?!*

He should be right at the top of the page where he always is. But no. Nothing. Has he deleted his profile? Why, though? He was an avid social media user. Always said it was a great networking tool for his personal training. So, where is he? Wait … What if something's happened to him? What if he's dead?! Oh, don't be a tit! He's probably just come off Facebook. After all, anyone who's anyone no longer uses it. It's as if Mother arrived on the scene and everyone else fucked off!

Bugger me, I've only been online all of forty seconds and already I'm being told to 'Be kind to others' by Carol Rogers, pub landlady at my old local whom, incidentally, stole all the cash from the Christmas savers club she once ran and has since made it her mission to educate everybody else on the basic principles of common decency.

'But we still haven't forgotten about Saversgate!', I almost type in the comments section of her virtue signalling bullshit … but don't.

I remember when Facebook used to be fun! My newsfeed used to be interesting, now it's all:

'Live, Laugh, Love' – Yawn

'Missing cat, last seen…' – Somewhere fucking miles away from me

Sponsored Ad

Righteous quote

Sponsored Ad

'Well done Charlie on your amazing first school report!' – He's five and will never see this, though?

Sponsored Ad

Someone's dinner

Righteous quote

Grinning selfie of otherwise haggard fifty-something-year-old with skin suddenly smooth as baby's arse – Wait till they see you in person, love!

Sponsored Ad.

Righteous quote.

'Look at this glorious sunshine!' – As well as my strategically-parked top-of-the-range car on HP.

Sponsored Ad.

'Like, comment and share this post to win…' – Something you'll never fucking win

Sponsored Ad.

Damn you, Zuckerberg! I mean, jeez, it's just a complete spamfest. No wonder Mr Wonderful's fucked off of it. Now the only other means I had of contacting him is, sadly, a no-go.

I *must* get that bloody sim card back. But how?!

Feeling doomed, I sit tapping my fingers

A KIND OF TRAGIC WEDDING

rhythmically on my knee, staring into space.

I can't very well call Brian to ask for my secret sim card. Nor can I ask for the bag after having made such a firm stand about wanting nothing his money paid for; I wouldn't give the git the satisfaction! Wait ... I've *got* it! Brian will be out on the golf course by now. I'll call the landline at his place and ask the butler if he can arrange for the bag to be sent on to Brooke's address.

Pleased with my genius thinking, I pull up my contacts list and make that call. It's perfect! At least it would've been if Duchess hadn't answered ...

'What do you want, Lizzie? You're wasting your time. Brian's never going to take you back,' she gloats nastily down the line.

'I'm not calling about Brian and I don't want him to take me back,' I snort. 'I'm calling to ask for a bag of mine to be passed on to me.'

'Don't you mean a bag of *his?* After all, he bought and paid for the majority of everything you had!'

'Excuse me? I have my own business, my own money and everything I need – none of which Brian Garcia has anything to do with!' I hiss.

'Hmph! Well, you're too late. Everything's been cleared out and taken away.'

'What?!' I gasp in disbelief. 'You couldn't possibly have cleared everything out in such a short space of time.'

'Are you calling me a liar?'

No. I was thinking more along the lines of a four-letter word beginning with 'C', but anyway.

'I'm just saying,' I continue, 'I've only just spoken with Brian about my stuff a little while ago. There's no way you could've cleared everything out that quickly,' I reason, battling to keep my cool.

'Well, it's all gone. Now, kindly don't call here again!' she barks, slamming down the receiver.

The line goes dead. She hung up on me! The old trout hung up on me!

Blood pressure surging, I grab a cushion off the sofa and begin punching its lights out.

'Gah! Stupid … bloody … bloody… shitting … bloody … bloody …'

'Have you ever been tested for Tourette's?!' comes Brooke's voice from in the doorway. 'Holy fuck! What are you doing?'

I freeze in my position, straddled upon the cushion I'm tearing limb from limb, bits of fluff raining down about the place.

'Killing Duchess,' I squeak, as though it explains everything.

'Come again?'

Before I can answer, my phone starts ringing with what my psychic sixth sense tells me is Mother's ring. Yep, it is and stupidly I answer.

'Hello?' I sigh.

'Oh, there you are! I've been trying to call you but you were engaged,' she pants.

Hm, not anymore … on *both* counts.

'Now, what's all this about the wedding being cancelled? It's not true, is it? Tell me it's not true!' she shrieks, hysterically.

Grimacing, I hold the phone away from my ear for the welfare of my eardrum.

'Well, I—'

'Because I've had that God-awful woman on the telephone positively delighting in telling me our plane tickets and accommodation have been cancelled and the whole thing's awf!' she continues in a slightly quieter tone.

'Mother, if you'll just let me speak!' I groan, feeling instant regret at having answered the phone.

'Well, go on then!'

'It's true, the wedding's off. Brian and I have split up.'

I gulp, looking in Brooke's direction for reassurance. Oh, but now *she's* the one who's engaged, head down with a silly grin on her face no doubt texting The Oracle ... *already*? She's only just left the git!

'Oh no! No!' Mother wails, as though someone has died a most tragic death.

'Well, *I'm* looking at it as a good thing, Mother. You don't know how hard it's been. How badly he's treated me lately and—'

'But he bought you the best of everything! He gave you everything you could've ever wanted and now you've gone and thrown it all away, you silly, silly girl!' she interrupts.

'No, he didn't, Mother. That's the whole poin—'

'Get on the phone to him, apologise for whatever it is you did and tell him he can count on you to be the perfect wife. Go on. Do it now!' she demands.

'Mother, it's over!' I insist firmly.

'NO! No, it's not over. It can't be. Everybody in my social circle knows about the wedding. Now they're all going to find out it's awf and I shall be a laughingstock. Just what am I going to tell everyone now? How will I ever show my face at the country club again?!'

The same way you managed it after getting nicked in public on my hen weekend?

Shaking, I hang up the phone and switch it off before the expletive-ridden tirade bursting to escape the confines of my gob gets the chance! I take a deep breath in and count to ten, thankful for the five-thousand-mile distance between myself and Mother – although, I cannot yet rule out her hopping on the next plane out here to march me by the ear to Brian to apologise for not being a size eight *or* disciplined *or* motivated enough for him.

'So, it's all out in the open then?' Brooke remarks, still gazing lovingly at her phone.

I nod despondently.

She looks up, eventually. 'Ah, Lizzie. I know it all feels really shit right now, but this is the beginning of a whole new chapter for you!' she soothes. 'Brian *totally* wasn't the one. You couldn't have possibly married him. Something had to give.'

I stare into space, not really sure of where it is I'm supposed to be and where I go from here.

'I'm a great believer in fate, Lizzie. When things don't work out, it usually means something better's just around the corner,' she adds.

Hm, so far the only thing I've discovered waiting for me around the corner is Dirty Barry and his stink. Not exactly what I'd envisioned.

'Look, why don't you just get on a plane and go find Dan,' she sighs.

'I can't just hunt him down like in some slushy bloody film!' I reason. 'We're five thousand miles apart. I haven't spoken to him in months. I can't just show up on his doorstep without calling and hope he's been waiting for me all this bloody time.'

'Why the hell not?' She shrugs. 'There's nothing stopping you now and you'll never know unless you do.'

She's right. I know she's right but …

'What if he's moved on?' I whimper, feeling nauseous at the mere prospect.

'Then at least you'll know, and you can move on with your own life.'

'But I don't *want* to move on without him,' I sniff, horrified at the thought of life without Mr Wonderful.

'Lizzie, book a fucking flight!'

Later...

'Hello, is that Jeff?' I enquire down the phone.

'Yah, speaking.'

'Jeff, it's Lizzie Bradshaw. You picked me up yesterday and drove me to the city?'

The line goes quiet for a few moments.

'Hm, Lizzie Bradshaw … I don't know no Lizzie Bradshaw,' he muses, clicking his tongue thoughtfully.

'Really? It was less than twenty-four hours ago. We were chatting about ...'

'Right, yah! You're the lady with the fiancé who doesn't like your farts! Er, sorry, sorry. Mouth running away with me again. I mean, you're the lady who walked out on her fiancé, right?'

'That's me!'

'Well, hey there! What can I do for you? You're not going back to him, are ya?!'

'No, no. I need that ride to the airport.'

*****

With what was the very last seat nabbed on a late-night flight to Heathrow and Cab Man on standby, I can now focus my attention on the more crucial elements of planning to ensure a smooth, stress-free reacquaintance with Dan. A reacquaintance wherein my knickers are highly likely to come off and, thus, requires the following:

    1. Underwear less frightfully shit.
    2. A neat little triangle like that of artsy nude model as opposed to flabby, angry ferret!

Hm, perhaps I should join Brooke in the waxed perineum club? Nah, bugger it. Too many folds. *Far* too many folds!

Similarly, a reacquaintance wherein my feet

are likely to wind up poking out the bottom of Mr Wonderful's bedcovers calls for TV ad-like, flip-flop ready, smooth, tanned feet with perfectly squared off toenails painted a high-shine watermelon pink. I peer down at my pale, flat feet, with zero arch, stubby toes and barely any nail to paint and conclude that I absolutely *cannot* rock up at Dan's place with Fred Flintstone feet. And, if I do, then I certainly won't be making his bed rock. Hm, short of a foot transplant, how else can I bring my grubby caveman feet up to TV ad standard?

Also to consider:

1. Fingernails bitten down to nothing like those of small child, due to recent stress
2. Legs white as moon and beyond hairy
3. Hair mad and Viking-like
4. Clothes have taken on Dirty Barry's stench
5. Must find passport which could be in one of twenty-two possible locations
6. Must ensure have chewing gum to hand in advance of possible fairy tale snog
7. Ensure have Kleenex to hand in case above is non-starter

Christ, that's some list to check off by this

evening!

'Er, how the fuck are you so bronzed?' I demand as Brooke saunters past the bedroom door like a sun-kissed beach babe despite the shit weather of late.

'Oh, it's this ace new tan I'm using,' she beams, proudly showcasing her flawless limbs.

'Ooh, could I give it a try?' I chirp, scary images of my white, bare arse in the wardrobe mirror surfacing in my mind. Yes, it's the size of Russia, but a tanned arse is nonetheless betterment.

'Sure, go for it.'

My phone suddenly pings with a text:

Your mother's going completely crackers. Currently hid up in shed if you want to talk about it? Dad x

'Hello darling,' he sighs, picking up my call moments later.

'Hi, Dad.'

'So, the wedding's off,' he says, blowing out a deep exhalation of breath. 'How are you feeling about it all?'

'Good in terms of it being over with Brian,' I reply, 'but if I'm honest, not so good in terms of where I go from here.'

'Well, I'd have thought *that* would be blatantly obvious, love,' he splutters in dismay, as though I missed a trick.

'I'm flying to London tonight, Dad,' I reveal after a pause. 'I should arrive tomorrow around lunchtime UK time. Please don't tell Mother, though. Not yet, anyway. I need to find Dan first and find out if there's any future for us and if there is, then ... well, I'll deal with Mother later.'

Possibly a little optimistic, but yeah.

'No, love. Of course, I won't say anything,' he assures. 'So, where are you staying?'

'Well, at Dan's place with any luck, after we, you know, reunite,' I tell him, trying not to think too hard about what that might look like being as sex-starved as I am. 'But I guess it all depends how things go.'

'I'm sure it'll be fine, love,' he soothes. 'I know how Dan felt about you. Feelings like that don't just turn off overnight.'

'I suppose so,' I agree, a hopeful smile etching its way up my face.

'Everything will be just fine, you'll see. And don't you worry about your mother, you just leave her to me,' he says, a little too over-confidently.

'Well, that's brave talk considering you're hiding from her in the shed as we speak!' I point out.

'Er, yes, well, er, it's easier this way, trust me,' he excuses. 'I know your mother like the back of my hand, love. She's like a toddler. Best left alone when she spits her dummy out, you know, to get it all out her system. Ah, yes. I've no doubt whatsoever she'll be back to slagging off that Delia Davenport and lording it down at the country club before too long, you mark my words!'

I sit perched on the arm of the sofa picking at my rough, neglected cuticles in angst.

'I don't know, Dad, she totally lost her shit with me on the phone earlier. I had to hang up on her before I said something I'd later regret,' I sigh. 'Besides, it would be all well and good her eventually accepting the wedding's off, but Dan would be a whole new bombshell. She hates his guts!' I remind him.

'Oh, she'll come round, love, she always does,' he dismisses. 'Dan's a good guy. She'll warm to him in the end.'

Although I try to keep as positive an outlook as possible in life, I somehow can't see Dan and Mother giggling over a Merlot together like she did with Brian. Only the rich and successful stand any chance of earning Mother's approval, and Dan is neither.

'This is your life, darling. You only get one shot at it. Don't waste it worrying about what other people think! You've got to look out for yourself and take charge of your own happiness. If *you* don't, you can be bloody sure no one else will,' Dad continues, sounding like a self-help book.

'But what if there's someone else?' I whimper.

'Look, it doesn't pay to go driving yourself crazy imagining all sorts!' He tuts. 'Just go and see how the land lies and tell him how you feel. You can either go for it or die wondering.'

'Hmm, you're right,' I concede.

'This has got destiny written all over it, love. This is meant to be, you mark my words!'

'Aw, thanks Dad. You know, no matter how bad I think things are, I always feel better for talking to you,' I confess.

'Well, that's what Dads are for,' he dismisses.

'No, I really think you're wasted in early retirement. You should clear out that shed and offer private life coaching from it. You'd make a bloody mint!' I enthuse.

A loud crashing sound follows.

'Dad? Dad, are you okay?!'

'Yes, fine, love. Just knocked a load of tools flying. Thought I saw … a false widow,' he stammers.

'You thought Mother was coming, didn't you?!' I tease, not buying it.

'No!' he lies. 'Doh, alright, yes! Let's bloody face

it, love, your mother's far more dangerous than any false widow,' he concedes. 'And in answer to your suggestion, I don't really see life coaching as a vocation. I can just picture all the troubled souls arriving for my therapy and leaving needing double after meeting your mother,' he scoffs.

We both break into simultaneous fits of laughter.

'Listen, good luck, love. Not that I think you'll need it. Take care of yourself and stay in touch. Call if you need anything.'

'I will, Dad.'

The afternoon sees my plans thrown off course somewhat …

Expectation: *Bronzed goddess fresh from Bahamas*

Reality: *Scary neanderthal!*

Verdict: *Livid!*

Brooke glances up from the sofa, instantly exploding into shrieking laughter.

'Have you been playing in the mud?' she finally asks.

'Hmph! So much for this ace new tan of yours,' I huff. 'I'm on a plane to London tonight and I'm not going to make it past fucking security now that I'm a whole new ethnicity!'

'Okay, so the colour guide's a bit dodge,' she laughs.

'This isn't funny, Brooke. What are you trying to do to me?!'

'Calm yourself, it'll wash off!'

Luckily, after practically scrubbing away an entire layer of my epidermis, I'm looking a lot less Stig of the Dump and a lot more bedroom-ready … at least it looks that way in this light. Could be a whole other story tomorrow!

*****

Late that evening, with everything packed, most items checked off that lengthy mental to-do list and my passport successfully retrieved, I zip up my case and drop it heavily down on the floor beside me.

'Ta-ra, Barry,' I chirp, tapping his tank, relieved to be getting some respite from the stench.

Lumping my case out of the bedroom and into the living area, I observe Brooke and The Oracle lounging on the sofa in an erotic clinch, eating each other's faces off, as per.

Rolling my eyes, I pause, waiting for an acknowledgement that doesn't come. An irked cough finally does it.

'My cab will be here any minute,' I announce, glancing at my watch.

'Okay, have a safe trip. Don't do anything I wouldn't do!' Brooke cautions jovially through a slightly insane-looking lipstick-smeared grin.

Hm. By the look of it, there's not a lot she wouldn't do. And where Dan Elliott's concerned, I'm no better.

'Call me!' she adds, grabbing Tom's face with both hands and immediately picking up where they left off.

A toot-toot alerting me to Cab Man's arrival outside spares me from having to witness any more of their pornographic petting … thank God.

Right, this is it. Time to find out my fate with Mr Wonderful.

Taking a deep breath inward, I lug my plain, non-designer case complete with missing wheel behind me toward the door.

Let's do this!

Chapter 14:

Roadblocks

'So, what made you change your mind?' Cab Man chuckles as we pull away in his cab en-route to JFK.

'Well,' I sigh before drawing a deep breath, 'I guess my mind was always made up, I was just scared to go for it.'

'He's the one, right?'

'I really do feel he is,' I conclude, my heart skipping a beat as though to confirm it.

'Gee, I only wish I knew what that feels like,' Cab Man replies melancholically.

'Well, you know when you've been driving for miles and miles and you suddenly spot the golden arches of McDonalds?'

'Hell yeah!'

'Well, it's like that, only on a way bigger scale,' I enthuse.

'Is that right? Well, thanks. I'll bear that in

mind.'

'You haven't found the one, yet?' I probe, regretting it instantly when he answers 'No' in a sad voice and I observe his puppy dog eyes through the rear-view mirror. Great. Now I'm vaguely entertaining the idea of adopting him!

'I thought I did once,' he says thoughtfully after a pause, 'but she left me for some Uber driver.'

'She did that?'

'Yah. I mean, what a kick in teeth, right? Of all the professions he could've had, it had to be my biggest competitor.'

'That's totally shit,' I sympathise, trying to be a good therapist instead of letting my mind wander to thoughts of being shagged senseless by Dan.

'I thought we were great, you know?' Cab Man witters on. 'On paper, we were a match made in heaven. We had the same tastes in everything. Liked all the same things. Then, all of a sudden, she started going out a lot. Said she was doing Couch to 5K. Hmph! Turns out it was more Couch to Having it Away!'

Aww, poor Cab Man!

I pause for a moment, trying to think of something worldly wise to say.

'Well, don't look back in anger,' I manage eventually, hoping he won't make the connection between my words of wisdom and the Oasis track. 'I mean, I'd look at it as a lucky escape,' I add quickly.

'Well, it sure knocked my confidence at the time,' he confesses glumly. 'Validation is like oxygen, right? We constantly seek confirmation from others that we're good enough. It seems there's this animalistic need for approval wired into us, so yah, when you get chucked for some douche with a man bun, it takes a lot of getting over.'

'Well, I think you're a great person and I've never liked man buns!' I declare as we draw up at the airport.

'Good luck with everything. I'll be rooting for you,' Cab Man tells me, slamming the boot closed and handing me my case.

'Thanks,' I chirp, 'and likewise! May we both be successful on our paths to true love.'

'I'll drink to that!'

*****

The plan was to sleep through most of my flight and quickly pass the long, seven plus hour journey back into the arms of Mr Wonderful, but it's a trying task wedged in a cramped standard seat with zero legroom, what with first class flights and complimentary pillows now a thing of the past. Added to this, my mind simply refuses to still, racing with endless thoughts – most of them X-rated.

Just as I'm sat picturing in great detail all the things I'd like to do to Dan Elliott, I feel a suspect familiar cramping in my lower tummy. No! Don't you dare! Don't you bloody well dare! Not today!

Cramming myself into the plane's toilet cubicle, which, by the way, I cannot believe affords passengers the space to even piss, let alone join the mile-high club, my heart sinks as my worst fears are confirmed:

Dear Lizzie,

Just when you thought you were in for a wondrous rogering, here I am!

Love Aunt Flow x

PS: This shall be the heaviest, messiest yet! Mwah ha ha!

No, no, no, no! Of all the fucking times it could choose to start. What are the bloody chances? I've gone weeks without any action. Weeks! A snog and a feel-up will simply not suffice!

Unable to believe my rotten luck, I begin kicking the door in frustration. Ugh! Ugh! Bloody, bloody, bloody!

'Everything okay in there?' comes a voice from outside.

'Oh, yes, fine, thank you,' I reply, all sweetness and light in a high-pitched voice while I roll off a yard of bog roll to fashion an emergency pantyliner.

Back in my seat with all former X-rated thoughts snuffed out, I begin wondering if Dad could still be right about Dan and me. Does this have destiny written all over it? Were the events of the past six months the universe at work, forcing Dan and I's paths back together? It certainly seems that way.

Somehow, I eventually nod off, only to be later woken by the most violent jerking ever. Oh, fuck! This is it, isn't it? The end is nigh! With the path back to Mr Wonderful now clear, it would be just my fucking luck to meet a sudden demise! To bugger off this mortal coil with so many words left unspoken and Dan never knowing the true extent of my feelings for him.

I clutch onto the seat in front for dear life as the plane lurches violently, making sudden breathtaking descents as if we're about to drop out of the sky.

'I don't want to die,' I wail, hysterically. 'It's not my time!'

A flight attendant hurriedly appears at my side.

'Ma'am, it's okay, it's just a little turbulence. Please calm down, you're going to cause a panic.'

A little turbulence? Pfft! What is this woman on?

'It's not! You're lying,' I wail, not buying it.

'Ma'am, please!'

I screech as the plane makes another sudden lurch. 'We're going down! I know it! I know it!'

'Ma'am, please! You're hysterical! This is your last warning!'

'You wouldn't even tell us if we were about to crash, anyway!' I shout, causing all on board under the age of twelve to begin screaming in tandem.

Next thing I know, I'm being forcibly restrained by two flight attendants.

'What are you doing? Get off!' I yell, thrashing about in my seat.

'You're being disruptive, ma'am. You've caused a panic so I'm afraid that in accordance with airline protocol, we need to restrain you.'

'How have I caused a panic? It's the bloody plan that's done that!' I shout in disbelief.

'You used the C-word, ma'am!' the female flight attended accuses in a hushed tone.

'When did I say the C-word?! When did I ever say the word c***,' I demand, earning myself several tuts and death stares from angry parent passengers. 'You can't do this to me! I'm a British citizen and I have rights,' I say, my protests falling on deaf ears. 'You're compromising the special relationship, you know. The PM will be furious. UK-US relations will never be the same again!' I bawl.

Then, as quickly as it started, the plane stops jerking.

Oh. It *was* just turbulence. And now I'm to be arrested at Heathrow. Fuck!

I find myself wondering how this could possibly have destiny written all over it as I'm later bundled off the plane by two policemen – along to the cheers of several passengers – and marched off to a side room in the airport.

'We're going to need to see your passport,' policeman one barks, rifling through my handbag while I sit having kittens about the crap that's in there.

Having eventually located it beneath a shit tonne of old receipts, crisp bags, sweet wrappers, and bus tickets, he opens it, glances at it briefly and shoots me a strange look.

'I'm not that photogenic, okay?' I huff, hoping my newly acquired tan doesn't look too David Dickinson in broad daylight.

The policemen disappear, leaving me sat in cuffs, staring at the clock, and wondering if I'm ever going to make it back to Dan. How long is this all going to take? I've never been arrested on a plane before ... Come to think of it, I've never been arrested. What now? Am I to be banged up in a cell all night? No. No. I'm a responsible adult and a good person – well, maybe not all that responsible, but still. It'll take them all of three minutes to see that I've no criminal record whatsoever and they'll be back in here undoing these bastard cuffs and apologising profusely before you can say arseholes.

Two hours and forty-five minutes later.

Thank Christ! Border Control has finally conceded that I'm not a terrorist and just a twat. I receive a firm warning about not using language that might cause distress onboard a flight in future and a confirmation that the C-word in question was 'crash'. Ah, shit.

'Do you need us to call anyone to arrange some onward travel for you?' policeman two asks.

'No, thank you,' I tell him, quickly deciding against having them call Dad who'll be mortified to learn that a second member of his family has been arrested this month.

'Then you're free to go, madam,' he declares, pulling a weird expression as I head out of the door.

Honestly! You'd think I was Julian Assange the way they've been carrying on. All I did was get a bit panicked on a plane, I mean, really!

Moments later during my scurry to the nearest toilet, a psychic inkling from somewhere at the back of my nut tells me I'm being gawked at. Turning slowly behind me, I quickly determine the inkling was spot on. Ugh! Yes, can I help you? I know I very probably look like shit, but show me one person who doesn't after a long-haul flight – judgemental bastards.

Oh, hang on a minute … Fuck! What if my arrest has made the news? Thanks to the internet, news travels faster than ever these days. I could be headlining in online news articles all over the place for all I know. Bugger. Hadn't thought of that! Oh my God, what if I am?! My blood runs cold as I picture Dan's shocked face stumbling across phone camera footage of me being bundled off the plane in cuffs looking a scruffy fucker.

I soon discover the true reason for my sudden acquisition of funny looks, and it has less to do with my badass arrest and more to do with the massive period stain on the arse of my ice blue jeans, which I discover as I take them down to pee. Hardly surprising considering the length of time I was cuffed – both in the air and on ground – but no! Oh, no!

Frantically, I battle to open my case within the miniscule space of the toilet cubicle, making a right racket as the handle smacks into the door and sides. Having fought tooth and nail to yank out a clean pair of knickers and a pair of black, skinny jeans, I turn to discover the empty toilet roll holder beside me. No! Fuck, no! Of all the effing cubicles I could've ventured into, it *had* to be the one with no toilet roll!

Now what? I'm in a right bloody mess – pardon the pun. What am I going to do? If only I'd packed those pocket-sized Kleenex tissues somewhere on my mental to-do list. Bugger. Well, I can't sit here all day, I've got to do something.

'Hello? Hello, could somebody help me please?' I call out, cringing at the sound of my silly little voice made all the worse by the toilet echo.

Silence.

'Hello? Could anyone help me please?' I try again.

Silence.

Concluding I must be the only one in here, I rise from the toilet seat, yank my soiled cacks and jeans up loosely and kick my case angrily out of the way before unlocking the cubicle door and peering apprehensively around it. Good! It's just me. I can just pop into the next cubicle and fetch some loo roll, I think to myself, moving to do just that.

A janitor chooses to burst in with a mop and

bucket just as I'm halfway between my cubicle and the next and my jeans and pants decide to drop to my knees, leaving my bare arse on display.

'Oh, o-oh goodness!' she gasps from behind me as I shuffle like the Duracell bunny into the next cubicle, slam the door shut and collapse onto the seat, my face beyond burning.

I spend the next twenty minutes willing the janitor to piss off and fishing my clean knickers and jeans out from the gap below the cubicle partition to next door.

Oh, why must these things happen to me? I'll tell you what, I don't know about destiny, I feel fucking cursed! This was totally not how it was meant to go, I think to myself on the way out of the cubicle, before jumping in fright at the sight of my flustered, dishevelled, sleep-deprived appearance reflected back at me in the garish lighting. Christ! I'm not doing very well on the path to true love, am I?

I do what I can with the only make-up products buried in the bottom of my handbag – a mushy broken lipstick adorned with bits of God-knows-what all over it and the very dredges of the last Touche Éclat my former budget afforded me – before standing back and making a final assessment of my appearance. Well, the Touche Éclat isn't quite the magic wand beauty editors would have us believe, but to be fair it was up against it with those dark circles and the newly acquired muddy green tinge to my skin tone. Ugh! That'll have to do! Too much time has been wasted already, I've *got* to find Dan!

*****

'Oh, hello. Could you tell me if Dan Elliott's about, please?' I ask at the Meet and Greet car parking cabin

'Dan Elliott? Nah,' the chap behind the desk replies brusquely.

I gawk at him open-mouthed.

'But he does work here, right?' I probe. 'And he is … alive?'

He looks at me blankly. 'Well, I should bloody hope so. He's covering my day off next week.'

I continue gawking at him for the solid confirmation I need that my prince is alive.

'He's not in today, darlin', on annual leave,' he adds, reaching to pick up the ringing phone.

'He's alive! He's alive!' I sing, turning and almost knocking an old man off his feet in my hurry to exit the cabin and get my arse in a taxi.

'Where to, love?' the driver asks, taking my case and loading it into the boot.

Dan House. Dan Lane. Dan Town. Dan County. Dan Planet. Dan fucking Universe!

'Er, Hackney, please. Crispin Road.'

Just as expected and in accordance with sod's law, the traffic is a nightmare. We've crawled all but a few metres in the last ten minutes, the UK summer sun beating down into the car making me even more hot and bothered than I already am thinking about Dan in the scud.

'Is there no other route we can take?' I sigh impatiently.

'No, love. This queue's going on for miles. We're going nowhere for the time being,' the driver replies, switching off the engine.

Typical. Bloody typical! This is fate fucking with me again. Honestly, it's been delay upon delay upon setback upon delay. Any other time and the traffic would've been flowing freely.

I give my pits an anxious sniff, anticipating the arising sweat patches and B.O should I be forced to remain in this greenhouse of a vehicle for much longer. I seriously contemplate asking the driver to risk life and limb getting out onto the motorway and fetching my roll-on deodorant from my case in the boot. Well, it's in his interests to avoid a car full of body odour, isn't it?

'Don't you have air con?' I ask, thinking it should be pretty standard in most cars in this day and age rather than the luxury it once was.

'Gas just went this morning, I'm afraid,' the

driver reveals.

Ugh. See, what I mean? What are the chances?! I'm cursed I tell you, cursed!

Suddenly, I catch whiff of a familiar pong. Either Dirty Barry's stench has followed me to the UK on my clothes, or the driver's farted, I think to myself, narrowing my eyes toward the back of his head accusingly. Hm, actually, it may be my breath, I concede, remembering it's been a while since my last drink – a single sip of the manky tap water provided by Border Control. Yep! It's me. Quick! Chewing gum. Now!

Sometime later, we begin moving. Halle-fuck-ing-lujah!

I put my window down and sit basking in the cool breeze with my head half out like an overheated spaniel, blissfully unaware of the effect it's having on my hair.

When the traffic builds up a few streets away from Dan's address and, not prepared to wait a second longer to reunite with my prince, I clamber out and insist on walking the rest of the way.

'Thank you, keep the change!' I trill, tossing a bundle of notes over his shoulder in a hurry with no time to worry about the random king of hearts playing card in among them. What the actual fuck was that doing in my bloody purse? Jesus, I'm like a walking odds and sods drawer!

Hurrying along the street, absolutely buzzing to see Dan again, I lump my case awkwardly behind me on three wheels, taking a wrong turn and winding up at the bottom of a cul-de-sac, looking about the place frantically like a pissed-off, lost sheep. Cursing, I turn and jog back up the cul-de-sac, puffing and panting. God, I hope nobody's watching!

Eventually, I arrive outside Dan's address, heart pounding. Oh-my-God, oh-my-God, oh-my-God! Here we go. This is it!

Lugging my case up the concrete steps, I pause by the door, peering at my reflection in the brass doorknob and clawing frantically at my hair when I find it to be unruly and Brian May-like. Taking a deep breath inward, I push the buzzer for Dan's apartment on the intercom and stand back in anticipation.

It bleeps for longer than usual before a young-sounding woman's voice answers, 'Hello?'

I go to speak but nothing comes out.

'Hello?' she repeats.

'Um, hi,' I squeak, like a disappointed mouse.

A pause follows.

'Er, hi. Who's this?' the confused voice enquires.

Awkward.

'I'm a … friend of Dan's. Is he home?' I ask, pulse racing.

'No, he's just popped out to get us some wine to go with dinner.'

Voice in head: *He's got someone else! He's got someone else! He's got someone else!*

'He shouldn't be long. Do you want to come up and wait?' the voice asks pleasantly.

'Er, no, thank you,' I reply, picturing Dan's face when he arrives home to find me lumped on his sofa making small talk with his new girlfriend. Part of me wants to go up and check out the competition, but I can already tell just from the air of sophistication in her voice that she's slimmer, prettier and a better shag. KILL! KILL! KILL!

'Okay. Well, can I take a message for him?' she asks helpfully.

'No. No, there's no message,' I tell her, eyes welling with tears as I turn and venture back down the steps, scurrying away as fast as I can before Dan returns and chances upon me crying my eyes out, lugging a skanky three-wheeled case at speed down his street when, as far as he's concerned, I'm pregnant in America about to get hitched to a billionaire!

Suddenly, my whole world is crashing in bits around me as my worst fears are confirmed. I'm too late. Mr Wonderful has moved on.

*****

'Lizzie!?' Dad gasps in shock, opening the front door and catching me just in time as I fall at his feet, sobbing my heart out.

He pulls both me and my three-wheeled case inside and quickly closes the door behind us. 'Whatever's the matter?'

'I-it's Dan,' I wail between enormous sobs. 'H-he's g-got someone else!'

'Oh. Oh, goodness,' he exclaims, patting my shoulder awkwardly. 'Come through to the front room, love. Your mother's down at the crochet club. She's not due back for another half hour at least.'

Finally, something's worked in my favour today.

I collapse into the armchair in a broken-hearted heap as Dad rushes to fetch the box of tissues off the coffee table. We sit in silence other than for the ticking of the grandfather clock and my hysterical sobs.

'Well, I really wasn't expecting to hear *that*,' Dad sighs eventually. 'I'm just as shocked as you are, love.'

'It's t-too late. He's moved on and it's too late for us,' I wail, dabbing my eyes.

Dad pats my knee. 'Oh, love. If he's moved on, then there's not much else to do but move on yourself.'

'But … But I'll never find anyone like him, Dad. He's my soulmate. I … I can't live without him!' I howl.

'Aww, look, love. I know it doesn't seem like it to you right now, but it's not the end of the world. Life goes on, I promise! You'll find someone else.'

'But I don't want anyone else!'

'Well, you won't for a while yet, love, but you will!'

'NO! NOOOOOO! NOOOOOOOOOOOO!'

'Alright, alright. Sorry. I'm sorry, love. That's not what you wanted to hear,' he guesses correctly, covering his ears having almost been half-deafened.

He falls silent, possibly deciding against risking putting his foot in it any further and sits holding me and stroking my hair while I cry it out, just like we did when I was little. Now here I am at thirty, wishing I was crying in his arms over something as simple as a grazed knee – as weird as that would look.

Before too long, the front door squeaks open.

'Ugh! Where did that tatty little case come from?!' comes Mother's plummy voice from out in the hallway. Sweeping into the front room, she stops dead in the doorway. '*You're* here!' she exclaims, hand-on-heart.

Hello to you too, Mother.

A long pause follows. I don't need to look up to know that she's busy mouthing 'Desmond, a word in your ear!' or similar to Dad.

Eventually, Dad gets up from the chair and the pair of them slink out into the kitchen talking in hushed voices, the odd disapproving gasp from Mother telling me she's been fully enlightened about my undying love for Dan Elliott and is predictably appalled. Eventually, they wander in from the kitchen with Mother displaying a dramatic change of tune – possibly as a consequence of still having a foot in the doghouse with Dad re her wild antics on my hen weekend.

'Well, I think we could all do with some cheering up,' she announces, clapping her hands together.

Yeah, no shit, Sherlock.

'Why don't we go out for a nice meal?'

'Not hungry,' I mutter.

'Now, don't be silly, dear. What's done is done. There's no point in going on hunger strike, you can worry about getting some weight off later.'

'I said, I'm not hungry!' I lie, stomach gurgling like a bitch from all those hours post-arrest without food.

'Come on, love. You've had a long journey. You've got to eat something,' Dad badgers. 'What say we try out that new restaurant that's just opened in town? It's supposed to be cracking!'

*****

'I wish you'd have tidied yourself up a bit, dear. Your hair's as wild as that big fellow's from the *Harry Potter* films,' Mother whinges while Dad shoots daggers from across the table.

Hmph! Hagrid-hair is the least of my problems.

'What do we have to do to get some service around here?' she complains, swiftly changing the subject.

'Oh, don't go making a fuss, Petunia,' Dad sighs. 'You can see how busy it is. They know we're here. They'll be with us as soon as they can.'

'Good evening,' a waiter says, arriving at the table sometime later to give out the menus. 'Apologies for the wait, we're rammed this evening.'

'No problem,' Dad assures as Mother pouts on, tapping her frosted coffee nails rhythmically on the table.

'Menu looks good!' Dad exclaims cheerily.

'Hm,' Mother hums, eyeing it suspiciously for lower class dishes and looking disappointed not to find any.

'Have whatever you want, love,' Dad winks, patting my hand and making me feel like a ten-year-old being treated to Wimpy.

I know he means well and he's only trying to cheer me up, but unless Dan Elliott walks through the door this second and snogs my face off, there's zero chance of that.

Voice in head: *Just think, the two of them are sat in his flat right now, drinking wine and eating his coq au vin ... and she'll be getting cock au Dan later on, too ... with her neat little triangle!*

If I'd have known my impromptu trip to London was going to result in me sat with my parents in a restaurant at my age, opposed to lying in Dan's bed getting a damn good seeing to, I'd have chosen to stay with Dirty Barry!

Later, as my giant Knickerbocker glory makes its way to our table – well, if I'm going to spend the evening feeling like a ten-year-old, then I might as well go the whole hog – I freeze in horror when I realise the waitress bringing it over is none other than Dan's sister, Lucie. Fuck!

'Oh, hello Lizzie, I thought it was you!' She smiles, looking at me and then at my dessert.

'H-hi,' I stutter, glowing bright red while transmitting telepathic commands to her subconscious that say 'You will not breathe a word to Dan nor any other members of the Elliott family about this massive, childish sundae!'

'I thought you were in America?' she says, her eyes discreetly dropping to my middle. 'Are you here with your husband?'

I shoot Mother a look that says 'Not a fucking word'.

'Er, no. We broke up,' I shrug, forcing a half-smile.

'Oh? I'm sorry to hear that,' she replies, grimacing awkwardly. 'So, have you moved back to the UK? Will you be bringing the baby up here?'

'Um … No, I lost the baby,' I mumble, biting my lip and looking away quickly. 'I fly back to the US tomorrow lunchtime,' I reveal, prompting Mother's head to suddenly shoot up in surprise, telling me she wrongly assumed my stay was to be permanent. Well, no point hanging around in Dan County prolonging the agony, is there?

'Oh, really?' Lucie exclaims, her expression telling me I could easily still pass for pregnant. Ugh, how embarrassing. 'Well, I'm really sorry to hear that too, Lizzie,' she says, awkwardly.

'How's Toby?' I ask, quickly re-routing the conversation.

'Oh, good! Good! Just as cheeky as ever,' she says, rolling her eyes.

Unsurprising.

'Lucie! Table twenty-two are still waiting for their bill,' a pissed-off looking colleague hisses in her ear as he passes.

'I better get on, we're rushed off our feet in here tonight,' she says. 'Was nice seeing you Lizzie. Have a safe trip back to the US,' she smiles over her shoulder before I got the chance to ask her about Dan's new squeeze. It's not that I'm a glutton for punishment, more that it would have been nice to have a name to put to the non-stop images of her dominating every second thought … and possibly a *real* image too after some meticulous stalking on social media! Hmph. I'll bet she's a Zara, a Savannah, or an Ayla – something trendy in any case. Oh my God, what if it's Kate Anderton, my imaginary childhood name? Pfft! That would be the sort of kick in the teeth I seem to attract.

'Why are you rushing off back to the US?' Mother demands to know as soon as Lucie's out of earshot.

'Because I live there, Mother.'

'Well, there's nothing left for you there now. I thought you were going to move back home to be closer to us. We aren't getting any younger, you know!'

Oh, really? What happened to the shot-necking, karaoke-killing, tackle-grabbing, policeman-stripping wild child in you?

'My business is over there,' I remind her sarcastically. 'You know, that small thing known as a livelihood?'

'Well, you can move it overseas, dear. Why don't you go UK-based?' she argues. 'British is best.'

'It's Brooke's livelihood too? She's my business partner?'

Her face drops in part defeat. 'Aren't you going to eat that monstrosity?' she asks, gesturing toward Mount Knickerbocker.

'No. Lost my appetite.' I grimace, pushing it away as visions of Dan's perfect new girlfriend run amok in my mind.

'Oh, what a terrible waste, dear! Think of all the starving children in Africa.'

God, I hate it when people make pointless points! How exactly is a rapidly melting Knickerbocker glory over six-thousand miles away in Britain going to help anyone?

*****

Opting to sleep in the single room, keen to avoid adding memories of Brian and his folded pyjamas to the mental torture I'm already enduring, I lie in the depths of despair, staring at the ceiling. How did it come to this? Only six months ago, two whole people wanted to marry me – the first turned out to be an arse, granted, but I still had more than one marriage offer. Now I have none. Nada. Zilch! It's as if I was one turn away from winning at Monopoly, then suddenly I'm bankrupt in jail. My fall from grace has been that bloody fast, I haven't even had the chance to process it!

This is *not* how it was meant to be. This is *not* how I'd envisaged winding up. If I could only turn back time, I wouldn't have left Dan and gone to America in the first place. Then we'd still be together. He'd still be mine. But sadly I don't have a time-travelling DeLorean. All I have is hindsight – which, by the way, is less "wonderful thing" and more giant effing handful of salt to my open wounds!

Ugh. Nobody will ever compare to him. Dan Elliott was perfect for me. A precious rarity. He knew me. The real me. He got me. He had this strange knack of knowing what I was thinking. How I was feeling. And, for my own sake, I shan't even go there with the lovemaking!

Why Did I let him slip through my fingers?! *Why?!*

I had him and I lost him.

Chapter 15:

Lost

'Rise and shine!' Mother trills, bursting through the guest room door and tearing open the curtains.

Or rather 'rise and decline' in my case.

'What time is it?' I croak, cocooned beneath the bedcovers with gunky, slitty eyes from crying myself to sleep last night – or this morning, I should say, with it having taken until well into the small hours for exhaustion to take over and force unconsciousness upon me.

'It's approximately 5.27am, dear,' she mumbles, craning her neck at the window to look down the street.

'5.27.am? What in the fuck?!' I gasp in disbelief.

'Oh, don't use language of the gutter, dear!' she scolds. 'Now, where's that ruddy postman? I've a bone to pick with him about all that junk mail he keeps putting through the door. There's an eye-level notice outside which clearly reads "No Junk Mail" and I'd love to know why he thinks it doesn't apply to him and his home improvement pamphlets!'

How do you even process all *that* at this ungodly hour? Moreover, how the fuck does Dad cope, I wonder?

'My flight's not 'til 12.30pm,' I hiss through clenched teeth.

'Come on now, you know what they say, the early bird catches the worm!' she sings, slinking out of the room.

Well, the early bird can piss off, I think to myself, slumping heavily back onto the pillow in readiness to steal another hour at least.

Minutes later, unable to ignore the pain-in-the-arse pigeon sounding off somewhere close by with its infuriatingly repetitive *woo-woo-WHOOs*, I admit defeat, storming out of bed for what is possibly the earliest shower I've ever taken in my life. Great. Well, since I must've gotten all of two hours sleep last night, even less the night before that, and I'll be getting even fucking less when I arrive back to my US sleeping quarters humming of turtle arse, the only thing *this* bird is likely to catch is herself in the mirror looking rough as arseholes.

I stand in a half-dead state of reflection below the jet of water, the voice in my head seeing it as an opportunity to start running off again:

Voice in head: *They were probably up all night doing it, you know! They'll be lying entangled in each other's arms after a long night of passion! She'll have the guns wrapped around her, making her feel all safe and loved. He'll be bringing her post-morning-sex breakfast in bed later on! IT SHOULD BE ME! IT SHOULD BE ME! IT SHOULD BE ME!*

*****

'Ah, *there* you are, dear. Breakfast is on the table,' Mother chirps, singing along to the kitchen radio in a suspiciously upbeat mood.

What's her game, I wonder? Last time I saw her sporting such a grin was when Fabio's knob was in her face.

'Now then, on reflection, I think it's a good idea for you to get straight back to America, dear,' she announces, suddenly.

Oh?

'You've changed your tune,' I remark, slumping down into a chair at the kitchen table.

'Well, you've no hope sorting things out with Brian while you're all the way over here,' she reasons, humming and straining the tea.

Oh!

Blood pressure surging, I whack the top of my boiled egg with my spoon as though it were

Mother.

'I've been thinking about it and I really think it's all just teething problems, dear. All couples have them and it's nothing you can't sort out. One of you just has to be the bigger person in the relationship, like I am with your fath—'

'WHEN ARE YOU GOING TO GET IT INTO YOUR BLEEDING HEAD THAT BRIAN AND I ARE FINISHED?!' I yell, slamming my spoon down on the table and striding out the kitchen, leaving her gabbling on about it being a widely known fact that even the Queen and Prince Philip had lovers' tiffs throughout their successful seventy-three-year marriage.

'Prince Philip was an alpha male, not some boring, business-obsessed, pyjama-folding, arse-head from hell with separation anxiety!' I shout over my shoulder on the way out the front door, slamming it closed behind me.

I stride huffily down the street, not knowing where I'm going and probably looking like some prat out power walking. Ugh, God! Quickly, I change my stride to one that looks more normal and less like I'm racing to the nearest toilet before I shit myself.

Letting my feet be my guide, I wind up sat on the grass in the cemetery, pouring my heart out to Nanny Bradshaw's headstone. I wonder what she would think of all the latest drama in my life.

What she would say if she were here? It's always nice to be comforted in hard times, but sometimes you just need someone with a lot of life experience to be blunt with you. To tell you how it is.

Distant echoes of her thick Cockney accent ring out in my mind:

'It's like I've always said, if yer want the rainbow, it's gotta piss it daan first!'

Well, in my case, it's never stopped pissing it down! I'm like a magnet for all things shit, constantly lurching from one disaster to the next.

I sit staring into space and listening to the birds tweeting. There's a certain essence of calm in cemeteries you can't find anywhere else, isn't there? Everything's so still. Quiet. Peaceful. Abandoning the split-second idea of taking a power nap in someone's family tomb, I revert my attention back to the long list of questions swimming around my head:

1. Other than for work, what am I actually going back to in America?
2. It's only a matter of time before Brooke and The Oracle move in together, where would that leave me?
3. Knowing how shit I did in my last flat, have I since acquired the required life skills to live alone in another country?
4. Are the bailiffs in America nicer than

their British counterparts?
5. How long will it take to get over Dan?
6. Will I ever find true happiness again?

Brainwave: *Shall plunge myself into work. Become a career woman fully invested in business with zero time for romance. Well, it seems to work for Brian? Ah, fuck. I'm a wedding planner ... romance **is** business!*

Well, that's it then. I'm doomed. Doomed to live out the rest of my days a sad cat lady, watching loved-up couples everywhere tying the knot and getting their happy ever afters while I languish on the shelf with Dan Elliott ever confined to history as the one who got away. All that's left for me to do now is adopt a load of cats, let them piss everywhere – including on me – or cut my losses and shack up with Cab Man.

'Help me, Nanny. I'm so lost!' I sob, head in hands.

A light tap on the toe of my shoe makes me jump and I look up to find a robin perched there. I freeze, wide-eyed, staring at it in shock. It stares back at me, cocking its little head this way and that. What's it doing? Does it think I'm some sort of weird monument?! Moments later it flies off again, leaving me open-mouthed but strangely reassured, as though an angel just whispered in my ear 'You're going to be okay'.

*****

'All set?' Dad asks as I lug my case downstairs.

'S'pose so,' I reply with a shrug.

'Now, take care, dear. Don't do anything silly!' Mother cautions from the hallway.

Bloody cheek! Although, yeah, I'd better remember to keep my gob shut in the instance of turbulence.

'I'm sorry I couldn't see you awf at the airport, but it's the community centre fete this afternoon and I'm needed on the cake stall,' she beams, patting down her hair with a snobby little smirk.

'It's fine,' I mumble, accepting a stiff, wooden hug. It's more than fine – in fact, it's a bloody relief.

'Call us when you land!' she trills, waving madly on the doorstep.

'See, told you she'd come around in the end,' Dad says, pulling out of the driveway.

'Except she hasn't, though,' I correct. 'She still thinks Brian and I are going to make it up and get back together.'

Let's face it, she's got more chance moving Fabio in with Dad's blessing than *that* ever happening.

'Well, at least she's in better spirits, makes my life easier,' he adds.

The iconic opening lines of Whitney Houston's "I Will Always Love You" ring out on the car radio, making everything ten times bloody worse as we drive to the airport in silence. By the first chorus, I'm silently howling, tears spilling down my cheeks.

'Get this crap off,' I half-laugh, half-sob, moving to change stations and taking us from Whitney to:

Roxette – "It Must've Been Love".

No!

John Legend – "All of Me".

Do one, Legend!

Adele – "Someone Like You".

Seriously taking the piss now!

Avicii – "Levels".

Crank the bugger up!

No matter how shit you feel, I challenge anyone not to get that "it's good to be alive feeling" when this song comes on. Even in my heartbroken, melancholic state, my spirits are already lifting. I turn to look at Dad ... Hello! The shoulders are going! The shoulders are going!

But not even the genius beats of Avicii can stop the sudden angst I feel as we turn off into the airport. Sensing my anxiety with his commendable fatherly sixth sense, Dad moves to turn the radio down.

'It'll be alright you know,' he smiles meagrely.

'Will it?'

'Yes, course it will!' he insists. 'People go through hellish situations in life and live to tell the tale. We humans are made to withstand a lot, you know. Just look at me, I've been putting up with your mother for decades,' he boasts.

There's still time for that nervous breakdown.

'Life doesn't always go as we'd planned, love, but it doesn't mean it can't still be great. You'll bounce back,' he goes on. 'Not right away, but you will.'

My staunch silence tells him I'm not so sure.

*****

'We're a little early,' Dad remarks, glancing at his watch as we arrive inside the airport. 'Fancy going for coffee?'

'Can do. Just popping to the loo, meet you in there,' I tell him over my shoulder.

I have some of my best thinks on the toilet. I can sit down with a dilemma and hear the answer in my subconscious mind before I even get up to flush, but that's usually concerning simple things like what to wear when nothing's washed, not how to cope after discovering your soulmate is shacked up with a bit of crumpet!

Collapsing heavily onto the toilet seat, the only thing I hear is a gasp from the next cubicle as a loud, involuntary fart escapes pretty much the second I relax everything to start the stream. Shit. I had no idea it was coming. Bugger me, I even fart when I haven't got wind!

Only when I'm more certain than not that the person privy to my bum notes has buggered off do I bolt out of my cubicle, give my hands the briefest wash ever and dash out the toilets like a whippet.

'I took the liberty of ordering you a cappuccino with extra chocolate sprinkles,' Dad announces jovially as I arrive at the table in the café. 'They're going to bring them over.'

'Cheers, Dad,' I smile, plonking myself down and pinching the rest of the carrot cake on his plate.

'Er, that's not mine, love,' he frowns.

I look at him.

'The table hasn't been cleared yet,' he enlightens me ten seconds too late as it's sliding down my gullet.

Ugh.

A lad who looks much like how I feel – grumpy – brings over our coffees.

'Mind you don't trip over your bottom lip,' Dad mumbles as he trundles off. 'Whatever happened to service with a smile?' he grunts, launching into a passionate rant about rip-off airport cafe prices before reverting back to the gloomy topic at hand: my getting over Dan Elliott.

'I know how you felt about him,' he says, squeezing my hand.

Oh? We're onto past tense already?

'But as nice as he seemed, Dan isn't the only fella on the planet,' he adds, 'and as much as I hate to use clichéd old sayings, it's true what they say about there being plenty more fish in the sea, love.'

Wow. For every worldly-wise bit of advice Dad has enthralled me with over the past six months, he's just gone and pissed it right up the wall with that one!

'I ... I don't want to talk about it anymore,' I dismiss, staring blankly at the table and recalling the moment I bumped into Dan here at the airport only six months ago, echoes of his voice still rippling through my mind from when he'd stood pouring his heart out in the rain.

'Everybody looks the same these days,' he'd said. 'Nobody's unique anymore, except you,' he'd said.

He'd seemed so sincere. The hurt in his eyes

that I'd moved on was plain to see – or so I'd thought. How can it be that six months on, he's moved on himself? Cosied up with some bird in his apartment. Cooking for her. Rushing out to buy wine. Probably giving it to her all night long. Cow! Either it's my own incredibly high expectations or might it just be that Mr Wonderful isn't that wonderful after all?

****

'So, this is goodbye, then,' Dad squeaks, eyes misting as we arrive before departures.

'Dad, don't start! I've cried enough already over the past twenty-four hours!' I groan, lunging toward him for a last fatherly hug.

I've never been one for goodbyes – possibly as a result of being left heartbroken and scarred for life as a child watching Dorothy bid farewell to Tin Man, Cowardly Lion and Scarecrow at the end of *The Wizard of Oz*. Funny, Dad often reminds me of the Cowardly Lion with his lack of balls where Mother's concerned and his big, cuddly exterior. Now as we stand here together, I feel as though I should be clicking my heels together and chanting 'There's no place like home'. How amazing would it be to wake up and find all this was all just a shit dream?

'It's going to get better, love,' Dad whispers, squeezing my arm. 'You take care of yourself.'

'And you, Dad.'

'Bye, love.'

'B-bye, Dad,' I sob, giving him one last glance as I walk away, my heart breaking just like the Tin Man's.

'Lizzie!' comes the echo of an urgent voice from behind.

I stop walking.

'LIZZIE, WAIT! DON'T GO!'

What the ...?

Slowly, I turn and look over my shoulder to find none other than Mr Wonderful racing toward me.

What?!

'Dan! W-what are you doing here?!' I gasp, hand clasped to my mouth in shock as he sprints over.

'I had to come and find you,' he pants, arriving in front of me looking as dreamy as ever in a tight-fitting t-shirt which showcases the guns beautifully. Oh my!

My stomach flips over as our eyes meet for the first time in what feels like an eternity.

'Lucie called, she told me everything,' he adds, taking my arm and ushering me away from the stream of passengers hurrying past. 'So, is it true?' he asks, gazing down at me with those piercing eyes of his, the long-dead butterflies in my stomach instantly rising from the ashes.

I nod, glancing quickly in Dad's direction to find him stood there looking just as confused as I am.

'Then in that case,' Dan says, fumbling in his jacket pocket before dropping straight to one knee in front of me - and the general public – 'Lizzie Bradshaw, will you marry me?'

Several gasps come from all around us, none bigger than my own, and a small crowd begins to gather.

Voice in head: *This is a dream! I really did take that power nap at the cemetery earlier and I'm about to wake any second now in some fusty bloody tomb!*

'B-but what about your girlfriend?' I frown, confused. I mean, we're living in modern times, but I'm not one for sharing.

'What girlfriend?' he frowns.

'I came to your place yesterday and a young woman answered. I assumed she was your girlfriend so I ran ... left again.'

He pauses in thought for a moment and then laughs. 'No! That was just Claire, my brother's girlfriend. They came to my place and we had dinner yesterday. She answered the buzzer while I was out getting the wine, that's all.'

All at once my face lights up like a kid's on

Christmas morning as it dawns on me that Mr Wonderful *hadn't* moved on at a rate of knots with someone slimmer, prettier and way better in the sack. He hadn't moved on at all. Cab Man, God love him, was right!

'Well? Do you fancy being my wife then?' he prompts, looking up at me from under sexy furrowed brows.

'Oh, go on then! You've twisted my arm,' I laugh, nearly twisting my own as I offer out my left hand toward him at lightning speed.

I stand beaming from ear to ear as he slides his Nan's engagement ring onto my ring finger ... and it gets stuck at the bleeding knuckle! I can almost hear the epic music sounding in my head grinding to an abrupt halt as the band refuses to budge another millimetre. Bugger. I go all stiff as I spy several onlookers standing around us with their phones out, capturing the moment.

'Oh, er. It's okay, they'll be able to do something with it at the jewellers,' Dan mumbles quietly, concealing it with his hand, rising to his feet and pulling me into an enormous hug as applause and cheers break out all around us.

I sink my head into his chest, not knowing whether to laugh, cry, or piss my pants – thankfully I wind up doing only the first two.

I peep over Dan's shoulder to find Dad doing the same, bless him. Turns out he was right after all; this *has* got destiny written all over it!

Chapter 16:

Finally

The venue stands ready. Well, as ready as it always is at the town hall registry office.

Old, mismatched furnishings? Check!

Crap old paintings? Check!

Musty smell? Double check!

But, more importantly …

Marrying soulmate and love of life? Checkity-check!

Which makes all of above deliciously irrelevant.

Despite combining the upheaval of selling my share of the business and moving back to British soil with planning Dan and I's nuptials, I've remained the essence of calm – worlds away from the last wedding I was organising. Correction, that Mother and Duchess battled each other to organise. It's as if everything has simply fallen into place. No shits given to colour themes, flower girls and pageboys, who wears what, who sits where and all that jazz. There are no frills, not even on my dress which is a simple, classy, off-the-shoulder white knee-length gown. No veil. No heart-stopping price tags, just straight off the peg and everything I need it to be rather than what everyone wants to see.

Dan and I were both in agreement that we wanted to tie the knot as quickly as possible and not spend an arm and a leg doing it. All the showy stuff is for everyone else's benefit. Today is about one thing: us. God, I love that word!

Who needs castles, Cinderella dresses and horse-drawn carriages? Marrying Dan Elliott *is* the fairy tale, and a far more spectacular one than any Walt Disney classic. But having said that, you should see the shoes. Cinders would be green with envy, but I just hope I can make it down the aisle in them without going arse-over-tit!

'Shall we?' Dad grins, turning and offering out his arm as we step out of my luxury wedding transport – a good old black London cab.

'Hell, yeah!' I squeal, brushing down my dress and moving my bouquet of pink peonies into place.

Linking his arm, we begin ascending the stone steps up to the open arched entrance doors of the building.

'Lovely day for it,' he remarks.

And it is. A backdrop of robin egg blue sky with the sparkling August sun adding the dazzling finishing touch to the best day of my life. Though, to be fair, any day's a good day to marry Mr Wonderful – even if there was a bloody monsoon.

'Listen, love,' Dad says, stopping and turning to face me part-way up. 'You look beautiful. An absolute picture. And I'm so ... I'm s-so p-proud of you,' he blubs, whipping off his glasses and dabbing at his eyes. 'Being here today, b-being here today is—'

'Alright, Alright! Look, I love you Dad,' I quickly interject. 'You've been an amazing support. I'm so lucky to have you in my life and I'll never forget how you were there for me through all this,' I tell him, pecking him on the cheek. 'But could we hurry the fuck up and get inside? I've waited my whole bloody life for this and I ain't waiting a second longer!' I demand, yanking him up the rest of the steps.

'Oh, right. Right, yes, okay, love.'

'Ah, you must be our lovely bride,' the co-ordinator greets us in an excited whisper as we enter in through the building. 'Everybody's seated and waiting.' She smiles. 'Follow me.'

Suddenly, I feel as though I might piss my pants at any second as we follow her toward the ceremony room. I stop short at pinching myself to check I'm actually here. I've had this dream a thousand times over, so it would be no surprise to wake entangled in both the duvet and disappointment. But no, this is real. This is all very real and it's happening to me. *Me*! Eek!

The co-ordinator pops her head around the ceremony room door and gives the nod, triggering the first orchestral notes of Etta James's "At Last"; a nod to both Brooke and the time it's taken to get my happy ending.

'Wait for the vocal, wait for the vocal,' I groan discreetly at Dad, yanking him back as he moves to walk in prematurely before my big moment at the drop of Etta's iconic voice.

Okay, deep breath … two … three … now!

As we enter into the room, he's the first thing I see, standing with his back to me at the top of the aisle. Dan Elliott. Dan the man. Danny Boy. The object of my affections and hijacker of my every thought. My stomach flips as he turns to face me, looking jaw-droppingly handsome in his trendy blue suit, that dashing smile I know and love instantly riling up the butterflies into a frenzy within me. I don't give much thought to how my ugly-crying face might look gliding down the aisle toward him right now. All I can think of is him. My soulmate, my world, my everything.

Two seconds later, Etta starts going apeshit.

'My lonely days … ely-days … ely-days … ely-days ... ely-days ... ely-days ...'

Bloody Brooke! Why did I trust that any CD in her collection would be in working order? I'll bet it's scratched to shit or covered in greasy fingerprints, or both. I clock her sat on the end of the left second row beside – and thankfully not on top of – The Oracle, looking sheepish. She shrugs back at me gormlessly.

I glance behind her to where Cab Man is seated beside Auntie Val. Well, I couldn't not invite him, could I? And by the look of it, it's a good job I did because he and the long-single Auntie Val seem to be hitting it off. He winks in my direction as I complete the rest of my trip down the aisle along to a soundtrack of Etta's stutters.

Dad pecks me on the cheek before shaking Dan's hand and making a sharp exit to the left, almost knocking off Mother's fuck-off great hat as he moves to take his place in the front row beside her. She races to adjust it, her face beneath it like a hard-boiled bollock.

The music shuts off – thank God – as I turn to face Dan. We lock eyes, a million tiny shocks surging through my body as though in confirmation that, yes, he's definitely the one. I've always known it deep down and, as I look at him now, I feel it more than ever.

'Hey, you,' he says, taking both my hands and holding them in his.

'Hey, you,' I blub, tears rolling down my cheeks.

'You look amazing,' he whispers, wiping my tears away and giving my hands a squeeze as the registrar gives the introduction to the ceremony, none of which is actually going in. I hear it, but it barely registers somewhere here on cloud nine.

I quickly find myself back in the room as Dan takes his vows.

'Do you, Daniel James Elliott, take this woman, Elizabeth Mabel Guinevere Bradshaw to be your lawful wedded wife?'

Thanks for that name, Mother.

'I do,' he smiles down at me.

Uh, my heart!

'And do you promise to love and cherish her? To protect and support her in good times and bad, forsaking all others for as long as you both shall live?'

'I do.'

'And do you, Elizabeth Mabel Guinevere Bradshaw, take this man, Daniel James Elliott, to be your lawful wedded husband?'

Of course I fucking do! Let me at him!

'I do.'

Eeeek!

Suddenly, what I can only describe as noise one might expect to come from a bereft seal breaks out. Good God, it's Dad sobbing like a baby! Now Brooke's joining in. Now Mummy Sharon's joining in. Now *I'm* bloody joining in – just when I thought I'd regained my composure.

The officiant pauses for as long as he feels able without risking running into the next wedding.

'And ... And do you promise to love and cherish him?' he eventually continues, raising his voice to be audible above the rabble. 'To protect and support him in good times and bad, forsaking all others for as long as you both shall live?'

'I d-do.'

'If any person present knows of any lawful impediment to this marriage, they should declare it now,' the registrar continues, invoking the odd few nervous laughs that follow that line at most weddings.

I glance over toward Dan's family on my right and catch sight of Toby, currently being smothered by his mother's hand clamped firmly over his cheeky little gob, thrashing about upside down on her lap. Good!

I turn my attention to Crabby Gran, sat clutching a cigarette she's positively twitching to get outside and smoke. Also, good!

And I needn't concern myself with Mother,

whom, after Fabio rocked up at the country club last month asking about that summer season, is very much back in the doghouse and on her best behaviour.

'Elizabeth and Daniel, your family and friends ...' the registrar trails off, raising a brow and clearing his throat.

Will not stop bloody crying?

'Stand witness to the life-long commitment you have both made to each other as we are gathered here today,' he continues. 'It is my pleasure to announce that you are now husband and wife.'

The room erupts into cheers and applause, along with the stadium's worth already sounding off in my head as Dan slides the white-gold wedding band onto my ring finger, leans forward just like in my many dreams and bestows that marvellous Disney Prince kiss upon me.

All that's missing is the glittering rainbow behind us and "The End" appearing in fancy looped text as the credits roll. But it's not the end, it's only just the beginning of the rest of our lives together and mine as Mrs Elliott, at long last.

So, this is what it feels like when dreams come true. This is what happily ever after looks like. I had often wondered...

And now I know.

About The Author

Gem Burman

Gem Burman is a British women's fiction author from Norwich, United Kingdom.

www.gemburman.com

Books In This Series

A Kind of Tragic

A three-part romantic comedy fiction series following the catastrophic life and daily struggles of plus-sized, potty-mouthed Lizzie Bradshaw and her brutally honest and hilarious experience of singledom, unrequited love and beyond.

A Kind Of Tragic

She's the perfect poster girl for how not to be and what not to do in life. Every day is an epic fail with calamity around every corner. She's a dreamer. A schemer. A complete chancer, totally winging it with no life plan and just hoping everything will somehow work out... but who says you can't be the world's biggest ninny and still win?

Lizzie Bradshaw's two great loves in life are donuts and Dan Elliott, her devilishly handsome co-worker and hers is one brutally honest and hilarious account of unrequited love that you do not want to miss.

Guys like Dan Elliott wouldn't usually look twice at women like Lizzie, let alone date them. But what if there was a way to change the odds and turn fate on its head, even with the supermodelesque new starter at work also vying for Dan's affections? (Cow!) It all seems too good to be true, but sometimes, all is not as it seems and Lizzie might just be about to discover she can have her cake and eat it; in more ways than one!

Disclaimer: not suitable for prudes, puritans, sticks-in-the-mud, goody-goodies, and/or the easily offended. May cause laughter-induced bursts of incontinence.

Warning: Page-turner. Highly addictive. May need to put entire life on hold whilst reading.

A Kind Of Tragic Motherhood

They say that marriage and children are the biggest tests of any relationship, but for Lizzie Elliott, nee Bradshaw, this must only apply to other couples; after all, she and Dan are soulmates and this is all she's ever wanted. It's a dream come true!
No. The biggest test of a relationship is when Margot Robbie's body double arrives into your husband's daily life in the shape of the breathtaking Amber Ross. She's fun, she's fabulous, and

she definitely doesn't eat yoghurts with a fork! But is she dazzling enough to take the shine out of Lizzie and Dan's marriage? With Dan growing ever more distant, it certainly seems that way. Something's off; something's changed. Is it all in Lizzie's head, or might it be that she doesn't truly know the one person she thought she knew inside-out?

With two under one's to care for, madder hair than ever, a flagging marriage to save, and no time to fart, this Calamity Jane is running on empty with a full swear jar!

Printed in Great Britain
by Amazon